Lester has never been okay with what his coven is doing. Attacking packs because they seek more power doesn't sit right with him, but he's just one man. What can he do against an entire group of mages who have more experience?

Mark tried to protect his clan, but he failed. When he wakes up after the fight, he's in pain and in a place he doesn't recognize. He's not surprised to find out the mages brought him home with them, but he is surprised by the gentle man tasked with taking care of him.

When Lester has the opportunity to get Mark away from the coven house, he does, but that leaves him without a home or anyone to protect him except for the pack Mark's brother belongs to. He doesn't know if he can trust them, but Mark still needs him, so he stays.

Lester and Mark have never allowed themselves to dream they could have more than what their parents wanted for them, but now, they have the opportunity to change their lives.

Will they take that chance?

Someone for Everyone

ISBN: 978-1-4874-4128-9
Cover art by Angela Waters

Published by eXtasy Books Inc

Look for us online at:
www.eXtasybooks.com

Someone for Everyone
Mayport Pack 4

By

Catherine Lievens

Chapter One

Something was happening. Lester didn't know what it was, but he could tell it was important. He knew better than to ask, no matter how curious he was. He didn't want to be cursed like he'd been the last time he tried standing up to the coven.

A piece of popcorn hit his forehead. He blinked and glared at his friend, Hannah. He wasn't sure how long she'd been trying to get his attention, but throwing popcorn was nasty.

Even though it got his attention.

"I asked what you thought of that," Hannah said as she pointed to the TV screen.

They were watching a TV show with people dancing around and singing. Lester was sure Hannah had told him what it was, but he couldn't remember, and he didn't know what she expected him to have an opinion about. She wouldn't take it well if he was honest, so he knew what he had to do.

"It was nice."

Hannah stared at him as if she couldn't believe what he said. Chris and Cole were sitting on the floor next to Lester's bed, and from the way they snickered, Lester knew it was the wrong answer.

Panicking, he stared at the screen for a moment. He needed to come up with something to say. "She looks great," he went with.

Hannah threw another bit of popcorn at his head. He tried catching it, but he wasn't fast enough, and it landed against his cheek.

"Will you stop that?" he complained.

"You're supposed to be watching with us."

"I'm sorry. I'm just distracted." And this kind of TV show wasn't his thing. He'd rather watch baking shows.

"Why are you distracted?"

"Can't you hear? Everyone's running around, and there has to be a reason for that."

There was always a reason for the coven to do something. Lester and his friends were never told what that reason was. Apparently, it was none of their business, because even though they were coven members and had been born into it, they were too young and stupid to do anything important. Lester might agree on the young part, even though he was twenty-six, but he wasn't stupid.

He definitely wasn't stupid enough not to know that the coven didn't always do the right thing. Most of the time, it was the opposite. Thinking about it made his stomach churn, and once again, he wished he'd been born in another coven.

"You need to ignore that," Chris said, reaching up and squeezing Lester's foot. "It won't end well if you try to stick your nose into coven business."

"But I'm part of the coven. It *is* my business to stick my nose into, isn't it?"

"Want to tell the elders that?"

Lester groaned and rubbed his face with both his hands. He'd never dare say something like that to the elders, and his friends knew it. The elders led the coven—and as far as Lester was concerned, they didn't do a great job—and didn't allow anyone to disobey their orders or even question them. Lester would know. He'd tried to ask questions many times, and every time, he was rebuked.

"I just don't like it," he declared.

"None of us like it," Cole said. His expression was sad. "It doesn't matter. We're not allowed to have opinions or participate, and I'm fine with that. I don't want anything to do with whatever they're doing tonight."

"They might be hurting people."

"If they are, I'm sorry for those people, but there's nothing we can do."

Lester slumped. He understood why his friends felt that way and would feel the same if he were smart.

But many people thought he wasn't smart. Some days, he had doubts, too.

He got to his feet. He could see the alarm in his friends' expressions, but he ignored them as he pushed his feet into his shoes. "I'm going to the kitchen to get something to drink."

"You're going to the kitchen to spy," Hannah hissed. "This isn't going to end well. You're going to get yourself killed."

Lester grinned at her. "I've been an idiot several times before, and I'm still here. I doubt they'll kill me just because I need something to drink."

Lester should keep his nose out of whatever coven business was happening and focus on his friends, on what they were watching, and on his studies. Even though he was twenty-six, he was still learning how to be a mage and control magic. That was why he was kept away from every important thing, or at least, that was what he'd been told.

He'd always wondered if there was something else behind it. Was that really the reason he was being held back? Did the coven want to test him before they welcomed him deeper into their midst? Or did they think he wouldn't accept whatever they were up to?

Lester shivered as he thought of the few people who'd done that. They'd left and had never been heard from or seen again. There were rumors that they didn't leave the coven as much as they were kicked out of it, and sometimes, they left feet first.

Lester swallowed as he left his bedroom. He didn't think he was about to be killed just because he was headed to the kitchen to grab a drink, but the other mages weren't stupid. They'd know he was trying to find information if he pushed too much, and they wouldn't take it nicely. He'd have to play up his innocence, which didn't come easy now that he was older. It would have worked if he'd been ten years younger, but his teenage years were long behind him.

When he reached the kitchen, he sucked in a breath, plastered a smile on his face, and walked in as if nothing was happening. A group of mages was scattered around the counter, leaning over something spread out on the surface. He tried to peek at it as he walked toward the fridge, and he might have managed if his mother hadn't got up from her seat to grab his shoulder. She tightened her fingers to the point of pain, and Lester sucked in a breath.

He didn't want her to know how he felt, so he continued smiling. "What are you working on?" he asked.

His mother gave him a shake before letting go. "None of your business. What are you doing here?"

"I was getting something to drink. It's allowed, right?"

"You were trying to stick your nose into this. You need to stay away. It's none of your business."

It shouldn't hurt, but it did. Lester had often been told something was not his business, and it always hurt. He'd worked hard, thinking that the coven would be more welcoming and include him once he was an adult, but they hadn't. They still saw him as a stupid teenager and didn't want anything to do with him.

He didn't mind. He might have wanted to be included initially, but now he knew that the coven was up to no good and wanted no part in that. He didn't want to be included. He just wanted to know what was happening.

He raised his hands. "I really just wanted something a drink. Hannah made us popcorn, and you know it always makes me thirsty. Can I get you anything?"

"Just take what you need and leave," his mother snapped.

Lester moved toward the fridge. He expected it to be over, but when he turned with a bottle of water in his hand, his mother was still staring at him. Knowing how powerful she was, it was kind of intimidating, but Lester had to behave as if everything was all right. He cracked the bottle open and took a sip, carefully ignoring the counter and the people gathered around it.

"What did you do to your hair?" his mother asked.

"I'm letting it grow." He'd wanted to do so since he'd been injured, but she hadn't allowed him to. She still wasn't happy, but Lester had decided he didn't care. He didn't want to see the scar on his face every time he looked in the mirror.

"It's too long."

"It's how I want it. You don't like it?" He already knew she didn't. She thought men should have short hair, especially her son.

"It's ridiculous. Fix it before I see you next."

Lester could have pointed out that he was an adult and could do whatever he wanted with his hair, but he wouldn't win this fight. It didn't matter, anyway, because both he and his mother knew he wouldn't fix it. It was perfect just the way it was.

He raised his water bottle at his mother in the mimic of a toast and turned around to leave. He still had no idea what was happening, but the coven was definitely plotting something. It was so secret that it could only mean it was important, which in turn probably meant someone was about to die.

Hopefully, that someone wouldn't be Lester.

"I'm worried," Rex said. "We all are."

Mark nodded. He knew what his friend was saying, and he agreed. The way his father was leading the clan would eventually bring them to the brink of destruction. It was a miracle that the clan was still standing, but if Mark's father continued the way he was, it wouldn't be for long.

"What do you want me to do?" he asked his best friends.

Both Rex and Charles stared at him from their side of the table. It was a bit early to drink, but they all had a beer in front of them. The sounds of the bar in which they were sitting were familiar and lulled Mark into a false sense of comfort.

There was nothing comforting about the situation.

Mark's father was driving the clan to destruction, and there was nothing Mark could do about it. To be honest, there wasn't much he *wanted* to do about it. He'd never wanted to be an alpha, but as Earl's firstborn son, he would be one. He'd been raised to become the alpha once his father decided to step down—if he ever did—and that was what he'd do. The few times he'd tried arguing, his father had let him know with his fists and fangs how displeased he was.

Mark had learned the lesson quickly.

At least Dustin was away from all of this. Mark should have done more for his brother, but he'd been terrified of what would happen to both of them if he did. Thankfully, Dustin's people had come to get him, and he wouldn't have to be forced into a marriage neither he nor the woman he'd been supposed to marry wanted.

Like all alpha offspring, they didn't have a choice. They did what their fathers wanted them to do, and that was that.

Dustin had escaped. Mark had been worried about him for a long time, but he didn't anymore. Dustin was safe and loved, and that was all he'd ever wanted for his little brother. He wished he could have the same, but he'd always known that wouldn't be in the cards for him.

So here he was, talking as quietly as he could with his friends and trying to think of a way to fix the terrible decisions his father was making. The clan had lost an alliance since Dustin wouldn't marry anyone, and their father had been so angry that he'd punched a new hole in the wall.

But soon his anger would vanish, and he'd start thinking about what he could do to fix this. Mark didn't think he'd go after Dustin again, which left only him.

He was already engaged. He'd seen the woman only once, but neither his father or hers cared about that. Like the marriage Dustin had almost been forced to go through with, this marriage would only be good as an alliance between two dragon clans. Mark had never had a choice, and he never would.

"There has to be something," Rex gently pushed. "He's your father, and you're the future alpha. He has to listen to you, right?"

Mark snorted. "Have you met him? He doesn't listen to anyone except himself."

"Which is how we got here," Charles pointed out. "He's pissing off too many people. Something's going to break, and the clan will pay for it."

Mark raked a hand through his short hair. His friends were right, but what was he supposed to do? He might be the future alpha, but he didn't have any real power. His father had made sure of that. He might want Mark to take his place once he was gone, but he had no plans to die anytime soon. He kept Mark around because it was expected, but he didn't really care about him. As long as Mark was an obedient son, he was happy.

But he was the only happy person in town.

Charles and Rex looked at each other. They both had an expression that told Mark they were about to suggest something he wouldn't like. It made him want to get up and run, but his best friends were his only support. Dustin had been gone for a long time, and Mark had learned not to count on him. More than that, he'd never wanted to burden his younger brother. This mess was his to deal with as the alpha heir.

"Maybe you could take over before your father dies," Charles said, looking everywhere but at Mark.

"I'm not sure what you're suggesting," Mark said slowly, trying to wrap his mind around the words. He suspected he knew but didn't want to believe it.

Rex leaned forward. "Your father has been getting worse, and he's going to get us all killed. We need an alpha who knows what he's doing and who won't be focused on his personal gain."

"Then it can't be me, because I have no idea what I'm doing," Mark snapped. "I can't take his place. What do you want me to do, kill him? Because that's the only way he's going to give up his alpha position."

Rex grimaced. "I get it. You don't want to hurt your father, and I don't want you to have to do something like that, either. But you have to see that something needs to change. We're all in danger as long as your father is in charge. Any other clan could decide to attack us, and they'd win. Your father is frantic to build alliances, but he doesn't realize that his behavior means that his people don't want to fight for him. What's going to happen if we're attacked?"

Mark shook his head. All three of them knew what would happen. The clan would be decimated and would vanish.

Most of the time, he didn't think it was such a bad thing. The clan was rotten from the inside, and not only because of his father. His father's close friends were just like him. They took advantage of their power and treated most clan members as if they were nothing more than dirt on the bottom of their shoes.

That included Mark.

He got to his feet. "I have to go," he said.

"It's still early."

Rex was right, but Mark had had enough of this conversation. He loved his friends and was as worried as they were, but sitting at the bar talking over a beer wasn't going to solve anything.

"We can get another beer tomorrow," he promised.

He wasn't surprised when Charles and Rex got up, too. They stuck together, like they always had since they were kids.

They left the bar, and Mark took a deep breath of cold air. It made him feel better, but only slightly.

He had a duty to his clan and his people, even though he'd never wanted it. He didn't have a choice but wasn't sure he was strong enough to stand up to his father. Someone would have to do something eventually, but Mark didn't feel he had the strength to be that someone.

But he wouldn't have a choice, just like he'd never had a choice in his life. His father had always made the decisions for him, and that wouldn't change anytime soon unless Mark made it change.

How could he? What was he supposed to do? The only way to get his father to step down from the alpha position would be to kill him, and that wasn't something Mark was willing to consider. He didn't care for his father and hadn't loved him in a long time. He knew him better than anyone else did, though. His father was strong, and he wouldn't go down without a fight. He also wouldn't hesitate to kill Mark if he threatened or challenged him. He wouldn't care that Mark was his son.

Mark didn't care about that, either. He just wanted this mess to be over and for someone to solve all of these problems for him.

Lester stared out the window and squinted, trying to see better. For some reason, the outside lights had been turned off. It was almost as if the coven didn't want the people left in the house to see what they were doing, even though they were all part of the coven.

Was it because of Lester? Had his presence in the kitchen warned his mother that he was trying to find out what was happening?

He wouldn't be surprised. He was her son, after all, and even though there was no love between them, she'd raised him. She knew him better than anyone, and that included knowing he was nosy as fuck.

"I can't see anything," he complained.

"That's a sign," Hannah said. "It means you need to stop spying on the coven and come here to watch more TV with us."

Lester didn't look back. Instead, he squinted harder, then murmured a few words that grabbed onto the magic in his core and directed part of it toward his eyes. He wouldn't be able to keep up the spell for a long time, but it gave him the opportunity to see better for a few moments.

Someone had driven all of the coven vans to the front of the house. Coven members were climbing in. There were so many that it was clear that whatever was happening was big.

"Are they attacking someone?" he asked out loud. No one in the room could answer, but it didn't matter.

"Let me see," Chris mumbled as he pushed Lester aside.

Lester didn't allow himself to be moved too far. He and Chris stood shoulder to shoulder as they watched the scene outside.

"It sure looks like it's something big," Chris whispered.

"That's what I've been saying all along. I'm telling you, they've been planning this for a while."

"You're lucky your mother didn't do anything when you went downstairs earlier, but that's not going to last if you continue spying," Cole said.

Chris and Lester exchanged a glance. Chris might not be as convinced as Lester, but he was just as curious. He clearly wanted to know, even though he wouldn't do anything to stop any of this when he found out.

Lester wouldn't either, even though he'd want to. Whatever was going on, it wasn't good. If he had to guess, the coven was about to attack someone, probably a group of people. That was the only explanation for so many of them climbing in those vans.

Everyone was dressed in black, and some had their faces covered. It was as if they didn't want people to recognize them. That made sense since no one in town knew about them. Powerful spells hid the house, and while most of the coven members regularly visited the town to go to work and shop, they didn't mingle. Someone might still recognize them, and they didn't want any trouble.

Not beyond the trouble they were creating, anyway.

"Who do you think they're attacking?" he asked Chris.

"How many shifter groups are around here?"

Lester grimaced. It made sense that was what the coven was going after. They wouldn't be doing all of this if it weren't a big occasion, and that meant they were targeting a shifter group. "They're not going after the dragons, are they?"

Chris shrugged. "They might be."

The bigger and stronger a shifter was in their animal form, the more magic and energy they had. Sometimes the coven needed more energy and magic than they had, and when that happened, they had to use an outside source. A dragon shifter would be perfect, but they weren't easy to defeat, especially without killing them.

What the fuck were the elders thinking?

"I'm going downstairs to see if I can get more information," Lester said as he pushed away from the window.

Chris caught his arm. "You'll end up in trouble."

He was right, but that wouldn't stop Lester. "I just want to know what's going on. I'm pretty sure I saw my parents climbing into one of the vans, so they won't know I'm there."

"They always find out when you stick your nose where you shouldn't," Hannah pointed out. "I don't understand why this is so important to you. Why do you care? It's not like they're attacking someone you know."

She was right, too. Whatever the coven was up to, they wouldn't be attacking someone Lester knew, because he didn't know anyone outside of the coven. Even though he was twenty-six, he'd never be allowed a job outside the house. He'd been trained as a mage, and any job he could find would be through the coven leaders. His parents had promised that he could find something else once he was older, but Lester always wondered if that was true.

He knew he was a pain in the ass. He asked questions even when he shouldn't. He stuck his nose where it didn't belong. He wouldn't be surprised if the coven wanted to keep him under control, but if that was the reason, his friends would have a job outside of the coven, right? Unless they were guilty by association, and the coven wanted to keep them under their control the same as they did Lester.

Either way, none of them ever left the house. It always made Lester wonder what was out there and if he'd ever find out.

But that wasn't what interested him right now.

He left his friends in his bedroom again. He was cautious as he went downstairs, knowing that no one would be happy to see him. His parents were already gone, so he wouldn't have to answer any of their questions, but there were still people in the house. The guards would be there, as would a handful of others who kept an eye on the children, took care of the chores, and of course, the people who weren't trusted.

Like Lester.

He was glad not to be trusted. He didn't like anything the coven did, including whatever was happening tonight. Even without information, he knew they were going to attack a shifter group. He wasn't sure what they needed that power for, and they wouldn't tell him if he asked, but the coven always wanted more. The only way to get it was to harness a shifter's power, which Lester didn't approve of.

It drained people. Once that magic was gone, they were nothing more than an empty husk. They couldn't shift anymore. If they were lucky, they'd live the rest of their life as humans. If they weren't lucky and the mages took things too far, they died.

Lester was pretty sure most shifters would choose the second option. He'd never been able to shift, but he could imagine how agonizing it was to lose such a big part of themselves.

He wished he could leave, but he didn't have anyone or anything else. His entire life was here, from his parents to his friends to the only place he'd ever called home. If he'd had anything or anyone else, he'd be gone.

But he was still here and couldn't imagine that would change anytime soon.

He peeked into the kitchen, relieved and dismayed when he saw only a few people there. Most were cooking and getting things ready for when the coven came back.

He stepped into the room with a smile on his face. "Hey," he said as he went to the fridge.

"What are you doing here?" Jeffrey, one of the guards, gruffly asked from where he was sitting at the counter. There were no traces of whatever the others had been focused on earlier.

"I was just hungry."

"Take your food and leave."

Lester nodded and opened the fridge. He *was* kind of hungry, so he started gathering food. At the same time, he kept an eye on Jeffrey.

The guard was on his phone again. He barely looked up, even though he was supposed to be protecting the people left behind. Lester didn't think Jeffrey would care if any of them were attacked, so it wasn't a surprise.

"The house is kind of empty tonight," he said in what he hoped was a casual tone.

"None of your business," Jeffrey snapped.

Lester plastered his best innocent expression on his face. "So it's important. I mean, if it wasn't, you wouldn't care if I knew, right?"

Jeffrey narrowed his eyes and put down his phone. "Why are you here?"

Lester grabbed the closest thing from the fridge and waved it at Jeffrey. "Just grabbing some food." He glanced down. Yogurt. Great. "I just thought the house was silent, and I was curious. You don't have to tell me, though."

"Damn right I don't."

Lester sighed. He was still right where he'd started.

Mark hadn't gone straight home. After leaving Rex and Charles, he'd decided to take a walk. He would have flown, but someone would have noticed him, and that was the last thing he wanted. Instead, he'd gone deep into the forest for a bit of peace and a few moments of not having to think about the clan and what his father was doing.

He didn't have a solution. No matter how hard he thought about all of it, the only thing he could settle on was that he didn't want to be the alpha but would have to. It would be a long time before that happened, which was a relief, but at the same time, it made him feel powerless.

What state would the clan be in by the time his father died? Would there still be a clan? Mark should hope there wouldn't, but no matter how badly he wanted not to become the alpha, he didn't want anything to happen to the people who lived there. They were his responsibility, and he took that seriously.

Eventually, he made his way back home. He needed to get some sleep, and he was cold. His father would no doubt want to see him tomorrow to talk about how ungrateful Dustin was for leaving the clan and not agreeing to an arranged marriage. That meant Mark would have to get married soon, and he dreaded the day.

He couldn't even choose the person he'd spend the rest of his life with. His father had, and he didn't care that Mark didn't think he could ever love a woman. He might have been able to if she had the right equipment, but unfortunately for him and his future wife, she wouldn't. She'd have to deal with having a gay husband, and Mark would have to deal with everything that went with having a wife he couldn't love. His father expected him to have an heir, but could he? Did he even want children?

A loud explosion startled him. He jumped and tripped on a root but didn't give himself time to fall on his face. He was already running, headed toward the area of clan territory where the explosion had come from. He tried shifting as he went, but for some reason, he couldn't.

His dragon was still at the back of his mind, growling and fighting to get out. It was distracting, but no matter how hard Mark tried, he couldn't shift. He'd done this since he was a child, and now, as a thirty-six-year-old man, he couldn't anymore.

It was terrifying. It felt like part of him was locked away, and he didn't know how or why or if he'd get it back. What was he if he wasn't a dragon shifter? What good would he be to the clan?

Even more terrifying, was he the only one affected by this, or was everyone else?

The clan was under attack. Mark didn't need to see what was happening to be sure of that. How could they defend themselves if they couldn't shift?

It felt like it took him forever, but eventually, he burst into the clearing where his father's house stood. It made sense that was where the attack would be, and while it didn't look like the explosion had happened here, the fighting had already started.

Just like he'd dreaded, no one was in their dragon form. They were fighting in their human form, but the people they were battling had an easy time dispatching them.

Mark's eyes widened when a woman dressed entirely in black raised her hands. Blue light glowed from them, and with a movement of her fingers, the dragon who'd been about to attack her flew backward. He landed against the tree, and Mark heard the sickening crunch of his bones breaking.

Mark resisted the urge to rush over to see if the dragon was all right. He wasn't even sure who it was, because it was too dark.

Instead, he launched himself at the woman. She hadn't seen him coming, so he had the advantage.

He'd never killed a person. He'd never had to, and he'd been grateful for that. His father might bicker with pretty much every alpha in the area, but it was never that serious.

But Mark was trained. His father had wanted him to know how to defend himself, and he'd been working with the guards since he was a teenager. That meant he knew what he was doing when he grabbed the woman's head and twisted it sideways.

There was another crunch of bone, and her body dropped. The lights on her hands vanished, and Mark let go. Her body slumped on the ground, nothing more than a puppet from which Mark had cut the ropes.

But she was only one person. When Mark glanced around, he was stunned by the number of people attacking. They all had glowing hands in various colors, and things that shouldn't be happening were happening.

Who were these people? *What* were they?

Mark remembered stories from his mother and his grandmother. They would talk about magic and the people who wielded it. There were rumors about a bunch of them living in the area, but Mark had never noticed anything he couldn't explain, so he'd always dismissed them as stories.

Clearly, he'd been wrong.

He tried shifting again, but his dragon was out of reach, no matter how much it thrashed and demanded to be let out. Mark was going to have to do this in his human form, no matter how petrifying it was. He'd probably die, but he was ready to do so if it saved even one dragon.

With a roar that didn't sound anything like the one he could make when he was a dragon, he threw himself into the fight.

He knew what he was doing, which was the only reason he managed to get two of the magic users down in a row. His luck couldn't last forever, and he knew it had reached its end when he faced another woman. She raised one of her hands, purple light glowing from it. Mark launched toward her, but it felt like something grabbed him around the middle and squeezed. When he looked at the mage, he saw that she was squeezing with her other hand, and every time she moved her fingers, the same movement played out in Mark's body. It was as if she had a massive invisible hand holding him up.

Then dropping him.

The ground came at Mark too quickly, and he braced himself for impact. When he hit the hard earth, his entire body was jarred. His teeth rattled, and his lungs felt like they caved in. For a moment, the only thing he could see was stars. The night was dark, and they twinkled above him.

Was this the end? Was this how he died? He wished he knew why these people were attacking his clan. Had his father done or said something stupid again? Was he the reason so many dragons were dying around Mark? Mark should have done more. He should have taken down his father if that was what it took to keep the clan safe. Instead, he'd failed his people, and as he felt blood bubble on his lips, he knew he'd regret it for the rest of his very short life. He hadn't been able to do anything. He hadn't saved anyone.

He hadn't even saved himself.

The woman appeared above Mark. He tried to get up and defend himself, but a sharp pain in his side told him he wouldn't be going anywhere. That made the woman smile, and when she reached for Mark, he expected more pain.

"You'll do nicely," she said.

That was the last thing Mark heard before the darkness wrapped around him. He knew he shouldn't, but he welcomed it. He hoped his death would be quick.

Even though that wasn't what he deserved.

CHAPTER TWO

Lester paced the length of his bedroom. "I know what I saw."

Chris raised his hands. "I'm not saying you're wrong, but it doesn't mean you have to be involved. This isn't going to end well."

Lester stopped pacing to glare at his friend. "It's not going to end well for the poor people they captured."

"No, but who would you rather end up hurt? You or them?"

He was right. If Lester tried to do anything, he'd be punished. He didn't particularly enjoy being punished, but could he really stay back after what he'd seen?

He'd spent half the night by his bedroom window, staring outside. He'd seen when the vans had come back, which meant he'd noticed that several bodies had been taken out and carried inside. They were in the house right now, and he had no doubt that the coven was hurting them.

Who were they? What was the coven doing to them? Why did the coven need them?

"It's not right," he said as he stopped moving. "They're hurting these people."

Chris rubbed his face and looked at the door as if he expected someone to be standing on the other side, spying on them. Lester wouldn't put it past his parents, but he suspected they were too busy today.

"I agree it's probably bad, but what can we do? There are only two of us."

"Not four?"

Chris sighed. "Cole and Hannah want out of this place as much as we do, but I'm not sure they'll want to help if we try to free those people. They're scared, and frankly, so am I. I don't want to be punished."

Lester didn't want to do this on his own, but he wouldn't force anyone, and he understood what Chris was saying. He wasn't willing to get any of his friends in trouble. If something happened, he should be the only one to pay since he was the one pushing for something to be done.

He strode to his best friend and hugged him. "It's fine. You guys don't have to be involved."

Chris squeezed Lester. "You don't have to, either. You need to let this go before it ends badly. You don't know what the coven needs those people for, but I wouldn't be surprised if they hurt you to keep from making trouble."

He wasn't wrong, but Lester couldn't ignore this. He'd watched the coven hurt people and destroy their lives more times than he could remember. He'd always told himself that he was too weak to do anything and that it was none of his business, but he was a coward. Was he terrified they'd hurt him? Absolutely. Would it be enough to stop him? Not anymore. If someone in the house needed his help, he'd find a way to help them.

He'd have to do it alone. He'd never forgive himself if his friends were hurt, especially with how hard they were trying to keep him safe.

"I'll be careful," he promised.

Chris looked sad as he stepped away. "I know you will be, but I'm not sure it'll be enough. I'd beg you not to do this, but it would be useless."

"I'm sorry."

Lester truly was, but he had to make a choice. He could continue living his life ignoring what the coven was doing, or he could try fixing it. He was only one guy, and against the entire coven, he'd lose, but he didn't have to fight the entire coven. For now, he just needed to find out what they were doing.

It was clear that Chris wanted to stick around and force Lester to do the same, but eventually, he had to leave. His grandmother was one of the coven elders, and she took his training seriously. Lester was glad he wasn't in Chris's place. None of the coven elders were good people, not even Chris's grandmother. She never hesitated to hurt him if it meant he'd learn magic faster. He was a little younger than Lester, and every time he came back bleeding, Lester's heart broke because there was nothing he could do to help.

He'd checked the news this morning, hoping to find out what the coven had done, but there hadn't been anything. If they'd attacked a shifter group, the shifters would still be licking their wounds. The coven wouldn't have been obvious about what they'd done to avoid drawing attention, so there might never be anything, but Lester had to find out more.

That meant talking to one of the people who had been brought in.

He was terrified when he snuck out of his bedroom and made his way downstairs. He didn't want to be obvious, but he also didn't want to look like he was sneaking around and doing something he shouldn't—even though he was. It was a delicate balance, and he tried to obtain it by staying out of the main rooms and hanging around the hallways.

That was how he heard the conversation.

He was slinking past the living room when he heard two women inside. He paused, looking this way and that to make sure no one was around to see him. He didn't look inside because he didn't care who was talking. He just needed to hear what they were saying.

"I should have known those dragons were all smoke and

no fire," one of them said.

"I expected more resistance," the other agreed. "I mean, they're dragon shifters. Surely they could have fought harder, even though they couldn't shift."

"It was ridiculously easy. Who do you think is going to last the longest?"

The other woman laughed. "Want to take a bet? The elders won't go easy on any of them."

Lester didn't have all the information, but he could make a guess from what he'd just heard. The coven needed power, and they'd attacked the nearby dragon clan to obtain it. They'd brought in dragon shifters to use as magical batteries.

And they had every intention of sucking them dry and killing them.

Lester was horrified. He looked around again, not wanting to be in the hallway if anyone walked past or if the women in the living room came out. The stairs weren't far, so he quickly went back upstairs. During the day, most coven members were downstairs, so no one would probably notice him.

His foot was on the last steps when he noticed a door opening down the hallway, giving him pause. Someone came out carrying a tray containing healing potions and supplies, which meant that someone in that room was hurt. It could be one of the coven mages, but if a mage had been hurt, they would already have been healed.

That meant one of the dragons was there.

Lester had to do something, but what? He was horrified by what the coven had done and what they were planning to do. The dragons they'd taken wouldn't survive their time here, but the coven mages didn't seem to care. Even if some did, they wouldn't say anything because they were too scared of the elders and the people who supported them.

Lester was.

He wanted to see what was happening, so he carefully

walked toward the bedroom from which the mage had come out. There was no one around, but he double-checked before pushing open the door.

A man was stretched out on the bed. His naked chest was wrapped in bandages, some of them already tainted with blood. He was only wearing a pair of jeans, and he was unconscious. He looked vulnerable, which was odd considering he was a dragon shifter.

But the two mages downstairs had said that the dragons hadn't been able to shift. That meant they'd used magic to stop them from doing so. This guy wouldn't be able to shift ever again if Lester didn't help him. The elders wouldn't want him to be able to while he was here. They'd want him to keep his energy so they could use it, and he wouldn't be able to defend himself if he couldn't shift.

"What are you doing here?" someone snapped behind Lester.

He turned wide eyes to his father. "I was just curious."

Unfortunately, his father wasn't alone, which meant he'd have to do something. He couldn't allow Lester to sneak around and stick his nose into business he wasn't supposed to know.

Lester was never sure how harsh his father would be when he punished him. Usually, when he caught Lester doing something he shouldn't be doing and they were alone, he let him go after yelling at him for a bit. Today, he wouldn't be able to do that. Two mages were behind him, and they looked positively gleeful at witnessing Lester's downfall.

"You were curious?" Lester's father asked.

Lester had been, and it looked like his curiosity might be about to kill him.

Mark was in pain and had no idea where he was. It felt

impossible for him to open his eyes. He was conscious, but barely. He could tell he was on a semi-soft surface, maybe a hard bed, and that he didn't have a shirt on. He couldn't move, and when he tried, it hurt. He could feel the tightness of bandages.

Had someone found him after the fight? Had they rescued him?

Something told him that wasn't the case. He didn't know what had happened, but he was scared to find out. That was why he kept his eyes shut even though he was awake and listened to what was happening around him.

He'd heard the door open several times and could feel someone was in the room with him. They hadn't been there alone for long, and they were talking.

"I'm sorry," a man said.

From the sound of his voice, he was young, and Mark was almost worried that something would happen to him. He shouldn't care, because the guy had to be one of the people who'd attacked his clan, but he couldn't help it.

"You'll be sorry if the elders find out about this. You're not supposed to be here," an older guy said.

"I just want to help. I hate that the elders always keep me out of everything."

"What are you talking about, Lester?"

Mark was interested in finding out, too. It helped distract him from the pain pulsing in his ribs.

"I don't know why the elders don't trust me, but I want to show them they can."

"By sneaking around?"

"What if I take care of him? You won't be able to use him until he's healed, and I can help with that. I'm good at healing. It'll free the mage assigned to him for other things. I know the elders don't want to involve me, but I can show them I'm useful."

So Lester was one of the bad guys. Mark had suspected that since he was here, but he'd been hopeful that Lester might help him escape. Clearly, that wouldn't happen.

Mark was on his own.

"It's not a bad idea," a woman said. "The elders can be set in their ways, but we need the younger generation. Why don't you give him a chance? The elders don't have to know until the dragon is healed, and if he fails, the elders don't have to know."

"I'm not sure," the older man said.

"Please," Lester begged. "I'll heal him as quickly as possible. I'll show you I can do it."

"All right, but if the elders have anything to say about this, you'll explain what happened."

"I promise I'll do everything the right way."

Mark continued to listen, but for a long moment, nothing was said. He heard footsteps going away, and he wondered if everyone had left.

He was startled when a hand touched his, but even though his body's reaction was to shy away, he couldn't move. It was as if he was stuck, and he panicked, knowing he needed to move if he wanted to leave. He tried pulling away, wondering how the mages had tied him up because he couldn't feel anything around his wrists or ankles. As far as he could tell, his body was just lying on the bed.

But he couldn't move.

He opened his eyes, needing to at least be able to see. He was startled again when he found a young man leaning over him. His brown eyes went wide, and he jerked away, which meant that Mark couldn't see him anymore.

That didn't last long. The man reappeared, and Mark wondered about the scar on his face. It ran from the corner of his eye to the corner of his lips. Unfortunately, he couldn't ask. His mouth was as frozen as the rest of his body.

The man was younger than Mark by at least ten years, possibly more. His hair was auburn, and Mark wondered if it looked like fire in the sunlight. The smattering of freckles on the man's nose was adorable, but Mark had to remember that this guy was a mage. He might even have been there when the clan had been attacked.

"I didn't expect you to be awake," Lester quickly said. "Since you are, you need to listen to me. I want to help you. I wasn't there last night, but I know what they did, and I disapprove. The problem is that I'm one mage against the entire coven, and I'm young. I don't know if you heard the conversation just now, but the elders don't trust me. That means I need to be cautious, because if I'm not, they'll forbid me to come back, and being allowed to tend to you is the only way I'll be able to help you."

Mark continued staring because there was nothing else he could do. He didn't know what to think of Lester. Was he telling the truth? Mark had a hard time believing it, but he wasn't okay with how his father led the clan. Maybe the same went for Lester. Maybe he was in the same position as Mark. He didn't like what his coven was doing but was powerless to stop them.

Mark told himself not to hope he'd get out of this and not to trust Lester, but it was hard when he was in an unknown place, surrounded by dangerous people who were planning to hurt him.

Lester swore, then waved his hand above Mark's face. It glowed a soft orange, and suddenly, Mark could move his head.

"Where am I?" he croaked. "What's happening? Why did they take me?"

"You're at the coven house. They took you because they want to use your shifter energy, but they can't yet because you're wounded. It won't last long, but it should give me enough time to find a way to get you out. I know it's a lot to ask, but I need you to trust me."

It *was* a lot to ask, but it was the only way for Mark to get out of here. He doubted he'd get this kind of opportunity twice. If he didn't want to be used, he had to escape, and Lester was his only possibility to do that.

"Help me," he begged.

Lester's expression did something complicated. Mark was pretty sure that for a second, he was angry, but he was also scared. It made sense because Mark was terrified even though he didn't know anything about the coven. He hadn't even known they existed until last night.

"I swear I'll do everything I can to get you out of here, but I'm working alone," Lester said. "I need time, and that means they'll probably hurt you. I'll try to keep everyone away as much as possible, but most people here hate me. They won't hesitate to report me to the elders if it means I'll get punished."

The door slammed open before Mark could say anything else. Lester's wide eyes told Mark to stay quiet and act as if his head was still paralyzed. It wasn't easy, but he did his best to stop moving as Lester turned around.

"What are you doing here?" a woman demanded to know.

She was tall and blonde. Even though Lester looked like her, he also looked nothing like her. Her expression was hard and uncompromising, while Lester was gentle and sweet.

Lester waved his hand at Mark from behind his back, and Mark felt his face freeze. He hated it but understood it was the safest thing Lester could do for both of them.

"I'm sorry. I was curious, and I came in. Dad said it was okay for me to heal this dragon so you can use him."

Mark's stomach dropped. *Dad?* Did that mean that the older man Lester had been talking to earlier was his father? Had Lester been playing Mark?

"Why would you want anything to do with that animal?"

"I never dealt with a dragon shifter before, and I'm curious. I thought that since this one's wounded, he wouldn't be able to hurt me. It's the best way to study him, isn't it?" Lester had lowered his hand, and to Mark's surprise, he found Mark's fingers and quickly squeezed as if telling Mark not to believe what he was saying.

That was what Mark told himself. He couldn't stand the thought that Lester had lied to him.

He was Mark's only way out. Mark needed to trust him, even though he knew damn well he shouldn't.

Lester should have known his father would go straight to his mother. She was the strongest and most powerful of the two of them, and she always made the decisions regarding Lester. Lester had wondered many times if she was the reason the elders didn't trust him.

He wouldn't be surprised.

But he needed to convince her to allow him to stay. He wanted to help the dragon, and he couldn't do it if he had to sneak in and out. If he wanted to get the dragon out, he'd need to heal him enough that he could walk, and that would only be the beginning. They had to devise a plan, meaning they needed time.

Lester's mother stared at him, and he could tell from her expression that she didn't believe him. She was right not to. He was lying to her. He didn't want to study the dragon. He wanted to help him.

But he'd appealed to her thirst for power and knowledge. She'd always wanted Lester to be more like her, even though she'd never given him the opportunity. She could forbid him to come back to this bedroom, but something told him she wouldn't.

"You want to study him?" she asked.

Hoping he was at least halfway to convincing her, Lester nodded. "I want to impress the elders. I don't know what they have against me, but I need to do more. The only way to do that is to be involved, and since no one will allow me to be, this is what I thought of. The elders don't have to know until the dragon is ready to use. Maybe they'll be impressed by how quickly I heal him, and I can even study him. When will I get another opportunity like this?"

Lester knew what his mother wanted most was recognition. She aimed to become a coven elder, and to do so, she had to impress the other elders. She had plenty of power herself, but showing the elders that her son was powerful, too, would reflect on her.

"Fine," she said eventually. "But don't talk to him. You're only here to heal him and study him. Once it's done, you'll tell me."

"You won't check in on me?" Lester was surprised she wasn't trying to micromanage him.

"I don't want anything to do with the beast until it's ready. I can check your work once you're done."

Lester was offended on the dragon's behalf. He might turn into a beast, but that didn't make him any less human. Lester wasn't about to tell his mother that. He'd get his ass kicked and thrown out of the bedroom.

She was already leaving. Lester watched her disappear into the hallway and took a few seconds to breathe in and out until his shaking legs got the message that he didn't have to run and that he was all right.

He'd done it. He'd found a way to get closer to the dragon. He was allowed to come and go from the bedroom, which meant no one would think it was weird.

He had to come up with a plan now. He couldn't rely on his friends, and while he was sorry about that, he also felt it was for the best. He didn't want anything to happen to them, and if anyone found out what Lester was up to, he'd be in a world of pain. It would be best if he was the only one who paid for this.

He turned back to the dragon and unfroze his face. The dragon reacted instantly, opening his eyes. He had to be frightened, and Lester's heart softened.

He could only imagine being in the dragon's place. He was unable to move, wounded, in a place he didn't know, surrounded by people who viewed him as an animal. He was going to be used as a battery and then killed.

It wasn't right. No one deserved that kind of fate, and Lester wished he could save all the dragons who'd been transported here. Unfortunately, he was only one guy. He wasn't even sure he'd be able to save this one.

"Why am I here?" The dragon. "Why me? Where's my clan?"

Lester didn't have time but felt the dragon deserved an explanation. "Shifters have a lot of magical energy. You need it to be able to shift, and the bigger your animal is, the more energy you need and have. The coven sometimes does spells that require much more energy than we have, and when that happens, we need to find an external source. That's why your clan was attacked. The coven elders plan on using you and your people to power their spells. They're going to use you until you die."

The dragon licked his lips. "Will you help me?"

"I'll try. I don't want to be involved with what the coven is doing, but I have no help. I'll have to do this on my own, and I can't fight an entire coven. I'll do what I can, though. I promise."

The dragon stared for a moment before nodding. "I'm Mark. If you manage to contact the clan, my father will help you. He's the alpha."

He looked so hopeful, and it broke Lester's heart. He didn't want to tell Mark there was probably nothing left of his clan. Besides, he didn't know for sure. He'd have to ask one of the mages who had been there, but he didn't dare. "I'm Lester. I promise I'll do everything in my power to get you out of here. In the meantime, you need to rest. They won't use you until you're healed, but it won't take that long."

"It hurts."

Since Lester would be the one to decide how to heal Mark, he could use painkillers. He didn't think any other coven members would have. He didn't want to use too much, though. He had no way of knowing when he'd have the opportunity to get Mark out, and Mark had to be awake when that happened. That meant finding the right balance. Lester wasn't sure he was good enough to do so.

But he'd try. He couldn't leave Mark in pain. "I'm going to go downstairs and get you some food," Lester told him. "You need to eat and rest to heal. Once I'm back, I can help you use the bathroom. Then I'll check your wounds to see what's been done and how I can help."

He could see some of the work the mage who had come out of the room earlier had done, but it was shoddy. Clearly, she didn't care about Mark and only wanted him to be healed enough to be used. That wasn't what Lester was aiming for. He wanted to heal Mark completely if he had the opportunity. It would make it easier to get Mark out.

He didn't know if he'd be able to, and if he could, what would happen after that. He didn't have a car and couldn't take Mark back to his clan, but if Mark was healed enough, he could shift and fly away. He could take things into his own hands.

Lester was still shaky as he left the bedroom. He forced himself to raise his chin and walk as if he had every right to be doing this. His parents had agreed he could take care of

Mark, so he would. No one would know that he had a secondary goal until Mark ran. Hopefully, they'd never find out Lester was involved, because they'd punish him if they did.

For once, Lester was glad everyone stayed away from him when he walked into the kitchen. It was full of people today, and all of them were talking about the attack last night and the dragons they'd brought home. It broke Lester's heart, but he couldn't help all of them, no matter how much he wanted to. Maybe once Mark was free, he could get his father and what remained of his clan to rescue their people. Lester didn't think they'd win against the coven, but they could still try.

But first, Mark needed to heal. Lester had to be as cautious and thorough as he could. It felt like an impossible task, but he was stubborn, and he was doing the right thing. The good guys didn't always win, but Lester told himself they would this time.

They had to.

Mark wasn't sure how long Lester was gone. The mage had frozen him again, and Mark loathed the feeling of not being able to move. He couldn't even open his eyes. It was like being paralyzed while being able to hear everything that was happening around him, and it was horrifying. It made him want to buck against the magic holding him in place and scream, but even if he tried, he wouldn't be able to.

He was stuck. The mages could do whatever they wanted to him, and he wouldn't be able to fight.

The sound of the door opening and closing made him tense. He waited, and as soon as he felt that his body could move, he jerked upward. He was ready to defend himself, but the pain took him down, and he flopped back against the pillow. It was good that the man standing by the bed was Lester, not another mage.

Mark didn't trust Lester, but he was the only one willing to help him, so he'd have to. He didn't have a choice.

"Don't do that," Lester scolded. "You're going to hurt yourself even worse than you already are, and that's not what we want."

Mark groaned, but he couldn't stop moving. He didn't want to now that he could again. He pushed himself into a sitting position again, more carefully this time. Lester was by his side instantly, helping him and putting pillows behind his back. He behaved as if this was normal, even though he knew that Mark was a dragon shifter and could eat him in one bite.

Not that Mark had enough energy or strength to shift. He wasn't even sure he'd be able to if he tried. What if the mages still had that spell on him that had prevented him and the clan from shifting?

At least it made sense now. Mark felt better knowing why he couldn't shift, but it still freaked him out. It wasn't natural not to be able to let his dragon out. The dragon was pissed and pushing forward, wanting to burst out so he could get them out of there, but Mark gently pushed it back. He'd shift eventually.

He needed to convince Lester to take that spell off him first. He also needed to heal, because he wouldn't be able to fly away if he didn't.

"I brought you food," Lester said as he gestured at the tray on the dresser.

Mark hadn't noticed it before, and his stomach growled at the smell.

It made Lester smile, and he went to grab the tray. "It's just leftovers. I can try getting you something better, but this is what was in the fridge for now. I also got you some water. You need to drink it because you lost blood."

It might just be leftovers, but it felt like a feast to Mark. He grabbed the chicken thigh with his hand and tore into it, almost growling as he did so. His side was painful, so he tried not to move too much. Every time he did, he winced. He kept glancing at Lester as he ate, but the mage wasn't doing anything. He'd gone to stand next to the window and was looking out.

"Why are you helping me?" Mark asked.

Lester turned to him. He looked so young, and Mark wondered if there actually was anything he could do. What if Lester had been sent here to fool Mark? What if Mark was supposed to start trusting him, only for Lester to use that trust against him?

"I don't have any real power in the coven, so no one listens to me," Lester explained. "They certainly wouldn't listen if I told them it's not right for us to grab shifters and use them to the point they die. No one deserves to die like that. No one deserves to die at all, but especially not for the gain of the coven. I wouldn't have been able to stop them from attacking your clan even if I'd tried, and I doubt there's anything I can do to save the other dragons here, but I can help *you*, or at least I can try."

Mark nodded, but how could he believe a word of that? He felt that he and Lester were in a similar position, which probably was why he wanted to trust the guy. They both followed the orders of someone they didn't trust or agree with. Both of them felt powerless to stop it.

But Lester was an enemy, and Mark couldn't just sit there and wait for the next thing that would happen. He was hurt and unable to shift, but that didn't mean he couldn't fight. If Lester truly was one of the good guys, he wouldn't hurt Mark to keep him here. After all, his goal was to get Mark away from this place.

But was it really?

Mark didn't know what to think. He wanted to trust Lester, but Lester was a mage, and mages had attacked the clan.

Mark hadn't seen Lester anywhere during the attack, but that didn't mean he hadn't been there or that he wasn't trying to get into Mark's good graces. Mark didn't understand why he'd want to do that when it was clear the mages were going to use him, but he didn't know Lester.

And that was a problem.

Mark continued eating and keeping an eye on Lester. He was free to move now, and while he was in pain, that didn't mean he was going to stay in this bed without trying anything. He needed to get out of this place, and since he suspected that the door was out, it left the window.

Thankfully, Lester had stepped away from it. He'd gone to the door and was listening as if he expected someone to come. If what he was saying was true, he needed the rest of the coven to stay away from Mark and his bedroom, but if he was lying, maybe he was waiting for someone to come and help him subdue Mark.

It wouldn't take much. Mark was wounded and in pain, and he couldn't access his dragon. Lester could probably take him on his own. Mark needed to do something. He needed to at least feel like he was trying to get out of there because he didn't know if he could trust Lester.

Slowly, he put down the tray, keeping an eye on Lester. The mage was focused on whatever was happening outside, so he didn't notice when Mark moved. Mark's every movement sent a burst of fresh pain running through his body, but he ignored it. He couldn't afford to let the pain win.

He was at the window when Lester finally noticed that he was trying to sneak out.

"What are you doing?"

Mark ignored him and attempted to open the window. He didn't have time to stop and explain that he didn't want to trust Lester because he could be one of the bad guys.

"You can't leave," Lester said as he rushed forward.

"They're going to kill you."

"Not if I shift and fly away before they can get to me," Mark snarled.

He pushed Lester away and wrestled with the window again. It was locked, but Mark was sure he could get it open.

"You won't have time to shift. You need to stay here, Mark. Please."

Mark shook his head and ignored him.

He shouldn't have.

He was still trying to open the window when he felt his body freeze. He just had enough time to turn to face Lester before his body started falling forward. Lester's hands were raised, and the soft orange light from before glowed from his palms.

Lester cried out and rushed forward. He managed to grab Mark before he could hit the floor, but Mark was too heavy for him, and they both stumbled. Mark tried to pull away, but he couldn't move.

Lester had frozen him again.

Mark was pissed. Was this proof that Lester wasn't on his side? It had to be. Why wouldn't Lester want Mark to run away if he wasn't planning on keeping him here? Had Lester lied all along?

Lester dragged Mark toward the bed. Mark dropped onto it, and it took Lester a lot of effort to get him back into the position he'd been in before, flat on his back with his arms by his sides. Lester was panting once he was done, which wasn't surprising, but the tear that rolled down his cheek was.

He wiped it away and narrowed his eyes at Mark. "You can't do that. There are spells everywhere that will alert the coven if you try to leave. I can counteract them, but I need ingredients and a lot of focus. Sneaking out the window won't help me, and it definitely won't help you." He hesitated and rubbed his eyes again. "I'm really sorry. I don't want to keep you here against your will, and if I could, I'd let you leave right now, but I need to plan. You have to be patient, even though I know it's a lot to ask for."

It was, but considering the position Mark was in, he didn't have any other choice.

CHAPTER THREE

Lester still didn't have a plan. He was wasting as much time as he could so that Mark would be stronger and he could come up with a plan, but so far, he had no idea how to get Mark out in one piece.

It felt impossible. There were spells over the house, so anyone would know if Mark were to leave. Lester could disable them, but he also had to get Mark out while making sure no one saw them and get him to safety, which he didn't know how to do. He'd barely ever been outside the coven house. Where was he supposed to take Mark?

If Mark was healed enough by the time Lester found the right moment to get him out, he'd be able to shift and fly away, but there was no way to know when the elders would lose their patience and start using him. If that happened, Lester would have to get Mark out, but he might not be able to fly, which would be a problem.

That was only one of Lester's many problems. His mother was watching him, even though she wasn't checking on Mark. It was as if she could tell Lester was up to something, which, to be fair, he was. He needed his mother to stay as far away from him as possible until he was ready to sneak Mark out of the house, but that wouldn't last forever.

This was going to be a disaster. Lester knew it, but he continued going through the days as if there was nothing on his mind. He spent a lot of time with Mark, even though the dragon was unconscious for most of it. He woke up to eat and use the bathroom, but his body was hard at work healing. He needed the rest, especially considering what they'd do once Mark healed.

Lester had been tempted to use more powerful healing spells, but he'd never used them before and didn't want to draw attention. It would be overkill for someone who was supposed to die in just a few weeks. The elders wanted Mark and the other dragon shifters they'd captured to be in good shape, but they wouldn't let anyone waste much-needed resources on them. As long as they were patched up, they'd be usable.

The dragons only had to be able to survive the spell for the coven to use their energy. It didn't take that much, although the healthier they were, the more energy they had. Lester suspected that was why Mark hadn't been used yet.

But that would change soon.

Lester carried the tray from the kitchen to Mark's room, surprised to see the door open. His heart jumped into his throat when he walked in and saw two mages on the sides of the bed, staring down at Mark. Luckily, he was unconscious, and Lester always kept him frozen when he wasn't in the room. He could tell Mark hated it, and he did, too, but it was for Mark's safety. Lester doubted the dragon shifter would be able to stop himself from moving if he weren't frozen.

"What are you doing here?" he asked as he put the tray down on the dresser. He recognized these two, and they always spelled trouble.

Amy didn't even look up. Her focus was entirely on Mark. Ambrose turned his attention to Lester, though. It made Lester feel like he was under a microscope and like Ambrose was wondering how to kill him. He wouldn't put it past the twins to do it just because they could.

"We have orders," Ambrose said.

Lester sucked in a breath. "From who?"

"The elders. They asked us to see if the dragon is healed

enough that we can start using him."

Lester wanted to scream, but he knew better. He had to make everyone think he was on their side. "He's not completely healed, but that's going to take some time," he said as if he didn't have a care in the world. "Maybe you should let him eat first. He'll be stronger after he has a good meal." Lester gestured at the tray on the dresser as if Ambrose hadn't seen it.

"It almost sounds as if you're wasting time," Ambrose drawled. "But I don't understand why you would."

Lester's heart raced. He couldn't afford for anyone to realize what he was doing. Unfortunately, it looked like that meant he'd have to allow Mark to be hurt. He didn't want that, but he didn't have a choice. Mark would be fine if the coven didn't take too much energy from him. It took weeks to take all the energy from a shifter, especially dragons.

"You can do it now," Lester said. "But I promised my mother I'd get him in top shape before he was used, and I always try to keep my promises, especially when it comes to my mother. You know how she is."

Ambrose grimaced. Everyone knew how she was.

Lester decided to push his luck. "He's not going to be in the best shape even after eating his lunch, but he'll have more energy to spare."

Amy suddenly turned her attention to Lester. He bit the inside of his cheek, trying to stay still and to keep a smile on his face even though he felt like screaming.

"Fix him," she ordered. "We'll be back in an hour. He'd better be ready by then."

Lester nodded and watched both of them leave. Amy had already dismissed him, but Ambrose glanced back as if intrigued and trying to find answers to whatever questions he was asking himself. Lester prayed the man wouldn't understand what he was up to. He didn't know what he'd do if

Ambrose did.

Die, probably. His mother would kill him for wasting this opportunity and lying to her.

Lester closed the bedroom door as soon as the twins were out of sight. He locked it, even though a lock wouldn't keep two mages away. He could do nothing else to secure the room without drawing attention, so he rushed to Mark's side and unfroze him.

Mark woke up with a jerk when Lester touched his shoulder. Lester quickly stepped back, giving Mark the time to remember where he was and that he wasn't in danger.

Not yet, anyway.

"You brought food," Mark said as he carefully moved into a sitting position.

"I did, but you won't like what I'm about to say."

Mark stared at him for a moment. "I take it you still haven't found a way to get me out of here?"

"I haven't, and there were two mages here earlier. They want to start taking your energy."

Mark paled, which was a feat because he was already really fucking pale. "How do we stop them?"

"We don't. You'll have to allow them to do it at least once. We're running out of time, so I have to stop waiting for the perfect moment to get you out and just do something."

"I could fight them."

"You'd die. You're not healed yet, and they have a lot of magic. I couldn't beat them, even though I'm a mage."

"I can't allow them to do whatever they want with me," Mark argued.

Lester didn't know what to do. He understood where Mark was coming from and why he wanted to fight, but the dragon shifter had to understand.

Lester stepped closer to the bed and grabbed Mark's face with both hands, forcing the dragon to look at him. Mark turned wide eyes to him, almost as if he expected Lester to *do* something.

"We don't have a choice," Lester said. "We'll have to allow them to do it at least this once. I'm still working on my plan to get you out of here, but my main problem is that I don't know where to take you once we're out. I can disable the spells all I want, but it'll be pointless if you can't fly away."

He let go of Mark's face and grabbed the tray. He placed it on the bed and ignored the way Mark was staring at him. He didn't want to lose him. He'd done so much to help the dragon, but it hadn't been enough. Was this really going to happen? Was Lester going to lose Mark?

He'd lose him anyway if Mark left, but at least he'd be alive. Hopefully, what remained of his clan was looking for him, and he'd be home soon. It was time for Lester to start doing more than healing Mark.

"I'll allow it once," he told Mark, looking him in the eyes. "After they're done, we're out of here."

Mark nodded, but Lester could see he didn't believe him. He probably wouldn't believe himself if he were in Mark's place.

He gave Mark time to eat, then put him back into his paralysis before the twins could come in. When they did, Amy looked delighted at the sight of him on the bed.

"He's unconscious again," Ambrose said.

He wouldn't have been, but Lester had used a spell so he'd be unconscious, at least for a little while. The pain would probably wake him, but he had a bit of reprieve in the meantime. "I told you he wasn't fully healed yet."

"There's a difference between not being fully healed and not even being able to keep his eyes open."

Thankfully, Amy interrupted them. "There's a new prisoner. Go take care of him, Lester."

Lester's stomach dropped. He'd wanted to be here to

support Mark, but he wouldn't be allowed to.

And who was this new prisoner?

Mark had noticed Lester use a spell to make him unconscious. He shouldn't have been as tired as he'd felt since he'd just woken up, but his eyes had closed as soon as he was done eating. He'd felt exhausted, although that probably had more to do with the fact that he was still healing rather than with Lester's spell.

But Mark was very much awake now. A bolt of pain centered in his chest had woken him up, and he would have flailed around if he hadn't been frozen. As it was, the only thing he could do was open his eyes, but he could only see the ceiling. He felt people around him. There was a hand on his arm and one pressed over his chest, just above the bandages.

The pain came with that hand.

Mark couldn't help it—he tried moving away and to let his dragon out, but nothing worked. His body didn't move as much as one inch. No matter how hard he tried, he wasn't going anywhere, and he definitely wasn't shifting.

He had to take the pain.

Luckily for him, he kept passing out. He could never tell how long he was unconscious before the pain woke him up again, but at least he didn't have to withstand it the entire time. The pain seemed steady when he was awake, so he imagined the same went for when he wasn't.

They were sucking out his energy. Lester had explained how it worked and why they were doing it, and Mark was pissed. How dare these people use him? How dare they think he was theirs to use?

He supposed he was, as long as he was paralyzed and in this bed. Lester had promised he'd get him out, but he hadn't kept that promise so far. Mark told himself it took time and that Lester needed to be careful, but it didn't help. Nothing would except for the pain to stop and for him to be free.

A woman's face appeared above Mark's. She grinned, but instead of being reassuring, the gesture was unpleasant and sent a shiver down Mark's spine.

"I always like it better when they're awake," she said. Her voice was soft and sweet.

She was terrifying.

The hand on Mark's chest pushed harder against him, and he knew it belonged to the woman. She was taking pleasure in hurting him. He wanted to shift and bite her head off, but he couldn't. He was stuck.

Mark had never felt so powerless, not even when he'd had to follow his father's orders. At least there, he'd been able to take time and space away from the situation. Here, he couldn't. Now that this woman was able to take Mark's energy, she'd do so until he was sucked dry.

Lester had explained that was what the coven was planning. He'd reassured Mark that he wouldn't allow it, but as he'd pointed out several times, he was only one man. What could he do against an entire coven of mages?

He couldn't even get the support of Mark's clan. Mark had no way to know what had happened to them, but he could imagine it wasn't good. The mages had captured several dragons, so there would be fewer people to look for Mark. Even more had to be wounded, or worse, dead. They wouldn't know where to look, even if there was anyone left. The clan hadn't been aware that a coven lived so close to them until they'd been attacked. Lester had explained that the house was hidden, which meant that Mark's clan couldn't find him.

The woman dug her fingernails into Mark's flesh. Even though he was frozen, he could feel the pain and screwed his eyes shut. His instinct was to scream, but he couldn't move his lips.

He wanted to die. For one moment, he felt it would be the best outcome. If he died, he wouldn't have to continue going through this. Lester wouldn't have to find a way to help him escape.

But Lester would still be stuck here. If Mark died, he wouldn't have any opportunity to leave. They hadn't talked much about that, but it was clear to Mark that Lester didn't want to be a part of this coven. He might have been born into it, but he didn't share their ideas or actions. He didn't want to hurt anyone, and he'd been wounded by the people who were supposed to protect him. It felt like a bad thing to abandon him, and since Mark had the choice to continue fighting, he decided he would. He might die anyway, but he wouldn't die without giving the mages the worst he had.

The fingernails finally unhooked from Mark's chest. He would have slumped if he'd been able to, but he still couldn't move, so his body stayed as it was.

The woman patted Mark's chest, and Mark's dragon recoiled in disgust.

"That was good," she said. "He's going to be an asset once he's better. I do think it's too early to do this, though."

"I'll let the elders know," a man told her.

Mark couldn't see them, but he could hear them. He listened to the door opening, then the voices fading. He didn't know what state his body was in, and he was afraid to find out.

Different footsteps rushed into the room—Mark recognized them as Lester's. Plus, no one else would have grabbed his hand as they leaned over him.

"I'm really sorry," Lester said as he squeezed Mark's hand with one of his while waving the other above Mark's body.

His hand glowed orange for a moment, and seconds later, Mark was free to move.

He didn't. He was in too much pain, so he only managed to groan and attempt to curl into a tight ball.

Lester didn't let him. He gently helped Mark onto his back again and stared down at his chest. Mark was afraid to look, so instead he kept his focus on Lester.

The man was incredibly handsome. Mark might have tried to get into his pants if they'd been in any other circumstance. As it was, they were both prisoners, so it wasn't the best idea.

Mark still wasn't entirely sure he could trust Lester. He only did so because he didn't have a choice, but what would happen once they were out of there? Would Lester betray him?

Why would he? The mages already knew where the clan was. If they wanted to attack again, they could do so without needing Mark. Lester had no reason to help the people who'd scarred him.

"You'll be all right," Lester promised. "Wait here."

Mark didn't think he'd be able to move even if he tried, but he was surprised when Lester didn't freeze him again. He went to the door, opened it, and peeked in the hallway. Mark watched him leave the bedroom and waited like Lester had asked him to.

He didn't have to wait long. The sound of footsteps came again. This time, when Lester walked in, he wasn't alone. Another man was with him, and Mark wondered who it was.

Especially when the guy rushed toward the bed and grabbed his hand.

"I'm so glad you're alive," the man said.

"I'm glad I'm alive, too, but who are you?" The man was as young as Lester, with curly blond hair and blue eyes that made him look like a Cupid. He was adorable, and Mark couldn't understand why he was there.

"I'm Wade, one of Dustin's friends. I'm here to help you."

Lester snorted. "He got himself captured. I had to let him

out of the room he was put in."

Wade glared. "That was just a mistake. Now, what did you plan to get us out of here? Because I'm not staying here one more second."

"We can't leave without a plan. It's too dangerous."

Wade smirked. "It's going to get more dangerous if I stay. My boyfriend will try to reach me, and trust me when I say that a bunch of mages won't be enough to stop him. That man is grumpy enough to kill them just because he finds them annoying."

Mark had no idea what to think of Wade, but if he could manage to get him out, he was all for it.

Lester gaped. Did Wade really think it would be that easy? If it was, Lester would have already gotten Mark out. They could do this, but Lester had expected to have a bit more time. "Unless your boyfriend can turn into Godzilla, he's not going to be able to defeat the mages."

"Then it's good he won't have to because we're leaving. You can help or stay. Either way, I'm leaving and taking Mark with me."

To Lester's astonishment, Wade moved toward the bed. Mark was still only wearing jeans and the bandages on his chest, but Wade didn't seem to care. He poked around the room until he found some spare clothes in the dresser, then helped Mark into a t-shirt. It would be cold, so Lester had no idea what Wade was thinking. He'd get Mark hurt all over again, and that wasn't something Lester was willing to let happen.

When Wade put Mark's arm around his shoulders and helped him to his feet, Lester knew he had to intervene. "You're going to get hurt, or worse, killed. You can't do this without preparation." Even though this might be their only chance to get Mark out.

Wade glared. "Watch me. He's already been through enough, and I won't let your people hurt him any more than they already have."

Lester hadn't known what to think when he'd stepped into the bedroom next to Mark's and found Wade waiting for him. Clearly, Wade had to be there for Mark. Lester had brought him food, hoping he'd found someone to help him. It was dangerous, but he'd asked for Wade's help, and Wade had been eager to give it to him, although Lester hadn't thought they'd do it right now. Wade wanted to get Mark out, and he was ready to fight.

Lester had been surprised when Wade asked about him. Wade could probably tell from Lester's behavior that he was terrified of being caught, and he wasn't wrong. Lester knew all too well what could happen if anyone found out he was involved in this, and he had no doubt someone would. He was the one in charge of Mark, and he'd been the one sent to Wade. It wouldn't take a genius to realize he was right in the middle of this, and he didn't want to think about what would happen to him when the elders decided to punish him.

Lester wanted to leave with Wade and Mark. He didn't know if he should or what would happen if he did, but the coven had never been a home. It was a place where he lived with the other mages, but they'd never felt like a family, just like his parents never had. Sometimes, he wondered why they'd decided to have him. Maybe he'd been an accident, or maybe his mother had wanted to raise him to be like her. If that was what she had in mind, she'd failed, which might explain why she disliked him so much.

But what was Lester outside of the coven? He'd only ever been a coven member. He'd barely seen the world out of this house, and not knowing what was beyond except through a TV screen was petrifying. It made him want to hide in his bedroom and never come out.

He might have tried if he hadn't known his mother would blast a hole through his door and come right in.

He watched for a few more seconds as Wade and Mark shuffled toward the door. They weren't going to get far at the speed Mark could sustain. Lester was surprised he hadn't fallen on his face yet.

He rushed forward to grab Mark's other arm. To his surprise, Mark gave him a small smile. He didn't argue when Lester wrapped his arm around his shoulders. Wade looked smug, and Lester had to resist the urge to glare back.

Wade didn't know how dangerous the coven was and what they'd do if they found out about this. They'd make Mark pay, but not just him. Lester and Wade would be punished, too, and it was never nice to be punished by the elders.

But Lester was involved now. This was what he'd been trying to do, and he couldn't step back. Maybe with Wade's help, he'd be able to save Mark, which was what he'd wanted all along.

Luckily, it was lunchtime, meaning most of the coven was busy preparing food and relaxing. Lunch and dinner time were when the house was mostly empty. Everyone gathered in the kitchen and dining room or disappeared into their rooms, so it would be easier to get Mark out.

But that didn't mean it would be *easy*.

Once they were at the door, Lester let Wade take Mark's weight. He opened the door and peeked out, ensuring the hallway was empty before returning to the other two. Together, he and Wade dragged Mark out into the hallway.

"The kitchen will be full of people at this hour of the day, but there's another back door," he whispered as they walked as quickly as they could while holding up Mark. "No one goes there because it's the mudroom, and it's really cold during the winter, so it'll be empty, but we have to get there."

"We will," Wade said. "I have faith in you."

Knowing that shook Lester to the core. No one had faith in him except maybe his friends, but even they hadn't been willing to be involved in this rescue. He understood why, but he still felt betrayed. Wade had only just met him, yet he trusted him enough to do this. Why couldn't Lester's friends feel the same?

"There will be a spell on the back door," he told Wade. "We'll have to take a moment for me to disable it, but once we're out, it'll be easier. There are spells there, too, but only around the house."

"Not in the woods?"

Lester shook his head. "I guess no one thought shifters would be able to find the house."

Wade grinned savagely. "They were wrong."

Lester couldn't imagine being as strong as Wade. He'd been taken prisoner, was in a place he didn't know, and knew what he risked by being here. If they were caught, the three of them would be tortured.

But that wasn't enough to stop Wade. He was there, dragging Mark down the hallway, convinced of what he was doing.

Lester had guided them toward the back stairs. They were rickety and in need of renovations, which was why Lester always took them if he could. It meant he didn't have to interact with the rest of the coven, which was always nice.

But since the stairs were barely used, they were kind of dangerous. It was especially dangerous for Mark, who wasn't steady on his feet. Wade and Lester had to be extra careful as they helped him down the steps. Mark's legs buckled a few times, but eventually, they reached the lower floor, and Lester breathed easier.

They weren't out of the woods yet, though.

He could hear people talking and laughing in the kitchen

and dining room. His stomach churned as if he was about to throw up, so he focused on keeping what little food he'd eaten for breakfast down as he led Wade and Mark to the back door. Once there, it only took a quick spell to disable the alarm on the door and push it open.

The three of them couldn't fit through the door at the same time, so Lester let go of Mark, and Wade helped him out. Lester hesitated, then stepped out after them, but he didn't go to Mark. He disabled the spell around the house, too.

He had a choice to make. Should he stay with the coven who hated and despised him, or should he give these people a chance? Why would they welcome him? He was a mage, a member of the group of people who had kidnapped Mark and tortured him. They'd attacked the clan and had killed countless dragons. Why would these people trust him? Why wouldn't they want to abandon him here to pay the price for letting Mark and Wade go?

Mark was in pain but was lucid enough to walk and listen to the hushed conversation between Wade and Lester. He'd kept his focus on them as they moved through the house, knowing he might faint if he didn't. He wanted out of this place, but his body refused to do what it needed to do.

But finally they were outside. Lester had moved away from Mark, and he looked up, trying to find him.

"Lester?" Wade hissed.

"I don't know if I can do this," Lester said. His voice trembled as if he was afraid.

Mark was pretty sure he was. Mark was terrified, and he'd only been here a short time. He could only imagine what it would be like for Lester to grow up with these people.

"What are they going to do to you if they find out you helped us escape?" Wade asked.

Mark didn't have to hear Lester's answer to know.

"They'll hurt me," Lester whispered.

He sounded like he knew what he was talking about. From the scar on his face, Mark suspected it wouldn't be the first time the coven hurt him.

He didn't want those people to hurt Lester ever again.

He still wasn't sure he could trust him, but Lester had been the only person who'd helped him while he'd been a prisoner. He'd fed and helped him in the bathroom, and while he'd also frozen him, he'd done so because he'd been forced to. He didn't deserve to be left behind.

But he had to be the one to make that decision, and Mark hoped he did so soon. They needed to get out before someone noticed they were on the run.

"Come with us," Wade said. "I told you I would protect you, and I meant that. Come on. We have to get to the nearest road before they realize we're gone."

Mark was surprised that Wade was so eager to convince Lester to come with them. Mark had gotten to know the mage, but Wade hadn't. How could he trust Lester enough to take him home?

Mark wasn't about to argue since this was what he wanted. The three of them needed to get out of there as quickly as possible. He'd shift into his dragon form if he could, but it was impossible. That spell was still there. Lester hadn't thought it would be smart to take it off because one of the other mages might have noticed, and even though Mark had hated it, he'd agreed. He didn't think he'd be able to shift even if Lester took it off, anyway. He was tired and in pain, and his legs barely carried him. He had to rely on Wade and Lester, something that wouldn't have happened if he'd been healthy.

"Wade," someone whispered from the bushes.

Wade frantically looked around. "James?"

He was going to get them killed. There was no way the

people inside the house couldn't hear him.

"We're here. The three of you need to hurry."

"I'm staying," Lester said.

He looked even more frightened now and kept glancing at the bushes as if he expected someone to jump out. He might not be wrong. since it sounded like the guy calling out to Wade was hiding there, and if Mark had to guess, James hadn't come alone.

Wade turned to Lester. "Shut up and come with us. We'll protect you. That's my boyfriend, and he'll make sure nothing happens to you, all right?"

Lester still didn't look convinced, but he nodded, and when Wade started dragging Mark toward the bushes, he followed. Mark wanted to keep an eye on him, but he couldn't focus on anything that wasn't shuffling his feet forward. He was sure he would faceplant in the bushes once they reached them.

Before they could, a man jumped out from the bushes, quickly followed by another two guys. Mark had no idea what happened, but he was wrapped in his brother's arms in seconds. He let out a sob, unable to deal with the emotion. Dustin cried out, but he didn't hesitate to hold Mark close.

Wade let him go, and Mark heard him talk to someone, but he couldn't focus. The only thing he could feel was Dustin.

He'd come for Mark. Even though Mark had mistreated him, he'd come for him. He was taking him away from the mages, and Mark couldn't even thank him because if he opened his mouth, he was going to start crying.

"We have to go," Lester whispered. "They're going to realize something's happened soon."

"Come on," Wade said. "Please tell me you didn't come on foot."

Mark wasn't sure who he was talking to, but it didn't matter. These people were here for him, and he was almost free.

"We didn't." That sounded like Wade's boyfriend. "The car is parked close by, so let's go."

Dustin and the other guy with him, whom Mark recognized as his partner, Houston, grabbed Mark under the arms like Wade and Lester had. They were taller and sturdier, so it was easier for them to tug Mark along, even though Mark couldn't help them much. He tried shuffling his feet forward, but his feet felt like they were made of lead. His entire body was heavy, and pain pulsed in his side. He wouldn't be surprised if he threw up, although he hoped he wouldn't.

Mark lost himself. He could feel his body moving forward, and since he was with Dustin, he knew he'd be safe. He focused on moving until Dustin and Houston finally stopped.

Mark blinked, returning to a reality he didn't like one bit. They stood in front of a van, and Wade was already opening the back door so that Dustin and Houston could get Mark inside.

Mark could have cried. Even though the van's floor was hard, it felt like the most comfortable thing he'd ever lain on. He allowed Dustin to move him this way and that until he was secure, and then, he let his body relax.

Doors slammed closed, and the van moved. Mark didn't need to see to know they were driving away. The vibrations reverberating through his body made him want to groan in pain, but he was too tired even to do that.

A hand on his chest made him open his eyes. It was much gentler than it had been when that woman had touched him earlier. He wasn't surprised to see it was Lester or to feel the pain fade. Lester had been taking care of him since he'd arrived at the coven, feeding him and using spells to keep the pain at bay. He was still taking care of him, even though Mark was free and with family.

"Better?" Lester asked.

Mark nodded and mumbled a *thank you*. Lester made to

move his hand, but Mark caught it. "The spell that blocks my dragon. Please," he asked.

Lester's eyes widened. "Of course." A soft orange glow appeared around his hand, engulfing Mark's, too. At once, Mark could feel his dragon surging forward. It wanted out, but Mark managed to keep it back, even though it used up the last of his focus. They were still too close to the mages. If he shifted in the van, they'd get everyone's attention.

"Who are you?" James asked. His harsh voice told everyone in the van who he was talking to.

Mark tried telling James that Lester had helped him when no one else would, that he needed to treat him well and that he wasn't dangerous, but he couldn't. His lips couldn't form the words, so he tried pulling on Lester's hand. Lester turned to him with a soft smile.

For a second, Mark didn't understand what Lester was doing. Then, his consciousness faded, and he knew that Lester was once again trying to keep him safe and from doing something stupid like attacking James because he was rough with him.

Dammit.

Chapter Four

It was hard not to feel judged by everyone Lester had seen since arriving in pack territory. They knew he was a mage and what mages had done to Mark. Lester hadn't even tried explaining he hadn't been involved in the attack or that he hadn't wanted to be, either. They'd believe what they wanted, anyway.

The ride back to pack territory the day Lester and Wade had helped Mark escape had been wild. Mark had been exhausted by the time they reached the van, and Lester had wanted to give him time to recuperate. He'd also seen how Wade's boyfriend stared at him, so he knew something was coming. That was why he'd used a spell to help Mark let go and slip into sleep.

That was when the interrogation had begun.

Lester sighed and pressed his forehead against the window. He felt like a tragic heroine in a movie. Mark had been spending a lot of time unconscious, both because his body needed rest and because Lester had kept him that way. He suspected that if he allowed Mark to fully wake up, he'd try to get out of bed, and his body couldn't take that yet.

He'd had to explain what the mages had done to a bunch of people, including James, since James was apparently high up in the pack security. He wasn't the alpha—Chance was much nicer than James—but he was important and in charge of pack security. Having Lester in pack territory meant James was involved, something Lester didn't love. He didn't understand how Wade could be with the guy, but he supposed a person couldn't help who they fell in love with.

He glanced at Mark. The dragon shifter looked better, although it would take some time for him to get fully healthy. Now that he wasn't stuck with the coven anymore, Lester had been helping him more than he'd been allowed previously. He didn't dare use spells he'd never used, but he could boost more power in the spells he did use than he had earlier. He'd fully healed Mark's ribs and the punctured lung that had resulted from that. He'd left the many bruises and scratches alone, but it shouldn't be long before Mark could go on with his life.

Where would that leave Lester? He'd done something he'd always dreamed of doing. He'd left the coven and was free of them. He didn't have to obey orders he didn't agree with anymore, and he never had to go back. He was free.

Except he wasn't. He'd left the coven only to find a new prison with the pack. James was there every time Lester left Mark's bedroom, looming as if he expected him to start using his magic on people. Maybe he didn't understand that wasn't what Lester wanted, or maybe he did understand and didn't care.

All his life, Lester hadn't been allowed to leave the coven house. Now, he wasn't allowed to leave Dustin and Houston's house.

That was where he and Mark were staying. Mark was Dustin's brother, so it made sense. What didn't was the reason Dustin had asked Lester to stay with Mark. Shouldn't he want Lester as far away from his brother as possible? He'd almost begged Lester to stick around and help Mark heal. For some reason, he trusted Lester. He didn't think Lester would hurt his brother or kill him.

At least that gave Lester something to do, although there wasn't much the rest of the time. He stared out the window a lot and people-watched, wondering what life that was for them. They were shifters. They belonged here and didn't fear they would be kicked out and end up alone without anything to their name.

That was Lester's position. He'd left the coven without anything except the clothes on his back, and he couldn't go back. They'd punish him if he tried, maybe even kill him. He didn't miss being with the coven, and while he did miss his friends and prayed the elders hadn't turned to them for answers, he'd always known his place wasn't there.

But where was it?

A soft knock on the door made him look up. He rose from his chair as the door opened, and Dustin peeked in.

"Good morning," Dustin said. "How are you?"

He was always polite, but Lester knew he really wanted to ask about Mark.

"He had a peaceful night," he informed Dustin. "I'm sure he's going to wake up soon. He's getting stronger every day."

Dustin came in, carrying a tray. Mark had barely done anything that wasn't eating or sleeping these days, so he'd appreciate finding breakfast ready when he woke up.

"I asked how *you* were, not how my brother was," Dustin said.

Lester looked away. "I'm fine." What could he say? He wasn't going to complain, especially not to Dustin.

From what Lester had gathered, Dustin was a recent addition to the pack. He didn't have as much power as James. He might say something to James if Lester asked him to, but what would be the point?

Dustin put down the tray and gestured at it. "I brought you breakfast, too."

Lester's stomach grumbled. "You didn't have to."

"Yeah, I did. You're taking care of my brother. The least I can do is feed you."

Lester was thankful but didn't know if he'd be able to eat.

He was too anxious.

He went to grab a piece of toast and nibbled on it. He kept staring at Mark because it was safer than looking at Dustin, but the situation was growing incredibly awkward.

"You know, I've been in your position," Dustin said. "Well, kind of. I didn't rescue anyone when I ran away from my clan, but I left because I couldn't stay there one second longer than I'd already been forced to. I disagreed with everything my father did and didn't want to marry a woman he'd chosen for me. The only way out was to run, and I left with barely anything."

Lester sucked in a breath. Maybe Dustin did understand him. It didn't change the fact that Lester was part of the coven who had hurt his brother, but it explained why Dustin seemed to have a soft spot for Lester.

"Your father never tortured anyone you cared about, though," he murmured.

"He tortured both me and my brother. It wasn't physical, but that doesn't mean it didn't hurt. Mark always felt he needed to go along with whatever our father said to keep him happy. He was raised to accept our father's every word as truth. He even accepted an arranged marriage."

Lester's stomach churned unpleasantly. "He's married?"

Dustin shook his head. "I don't think so. He wasn't the last time I saw him, and there hasn't been time for him to marry anyone since then. I know our father had arranged something, though. Mark would have been forced to go through with it if the clan hadn't been attacked."

Lester snorted. "You make it sound like we did you a favor."

"The coven destroyed the clan, and while my father was the alpha, most of the people who lived there didn't deserve that kind of pain. I hate what my brother has been through, and I hope he'll fully heal. Now that the clan is gone, though, he finally has a choice. He doesn't have to follow our father's orders anymore. He can decide how to live his life and who to marry."

Lester didn't understand how Dustin could think like that. He sounded almost happy that the clan was gone, but that didn't make sense.

Maybe it did. Lester tried to ask himself how he would feel if he found out the coven was gone. It might have been the place where he grew up, but it had never been a home, and the coven members had never been a family. They'd been people who had hurt Lester—including his parents.

He raised a hand and touched the scar on his face. Maybe he'd be happy if he found that the coven was gone. Maybe he did understand Dustin more than he'd expected.

"You won't be stuck in this bedroom forever," Dustin said gently. "James can be rough around the edges, but he's not a bad person, and he's not the one making decisions. Chance is, and I'm sure he'll come to trust you."

Lester wasn't convinced, but part of him wanted the alpha to trust him. Part of him wanted the pack to be a home and a place where he belonged.

He was never going back to the coven, but where did that leave him?

Mark's mouth was as dry as a desert. He smacked his lips, wondering if there was water nearby.

He opened his eyes to check. It took him a moment to recognize the bedroom he was in, and when he did, he smiled.

He was safe. He was with Dustin.

He tried sitting up, and like the other times he'd woken up, someone was with him right away. It had always been Lester, so Mark wasn't surprised to see him again. It looked like he spent a lot of time in the bedroom with Mark. Mark had wanted to ask him about it sooner, but he kept falling asleep.

His body was still recovering from several traumas. He'd been hurt in the fight against the mages, then again when that woman had stolen his energy. Mark wasn't sure which was worse, but the pain had come mainly from his broken ribs and punctured lung. When the healer had seen him, she'd been stunned that Mark had managed to survive.

It was all thanks to Lester. Mark wouldn't be here today if it hadn't been for him, and he didn't think he could ever thank him enough for what he'd done. Lester probably wouldn't want to be thanked, but that didn't mean Mark wouldn't try. He wanted to do something for Lester, but he wasn't sure what was in his power to do. He was healing and safe, but he wasn't home.

He was staying with Dustin, and they were spending more time together than they had since they were children. As they grew up, Mark had pulled away from his brother. He'd realized it would be best for Dustin if he kept his distance. It meant their father didn't turn his attention to Dustin too often, keeping it on Mark instead. Mark had been trying to protect his brother, but now, he wondered if he'd done it the right way. Maybe he should have talked to Dustin instead.

But all of that was in the past, at least for now. Mark would have to return home eventually, but he still had some time. He hadn't even talked to his father yet. He was afraid to.

His life might be painful, but it was also peaceful. He spent all of his time in his bedroom, sleeping and watching bad TV with Lester. If he could choose, he'd never want anything to change.

There was an entire world out there, and eventually, something would have to happen.

"Everything all right?" Lester asked.

Mark looked at him. He still wasn't sure he could trust the mage, but Lester hadn't done anything to hurt him. He'd saved him and spent time healing him and using that pain-killer spell so he wouldn't be in too much pain. He wouldn't have done that if he was still working with the coven, right?

Sometimes, Mark couldn't help but wonder. What if Lester had been sent to spy on the pack? Maybe someone had realized that Mark was his father's heir and had decided to use him as a ruse.

But that didn't make sense. Even if anyone had known who Mark was, they couldn't have linked him to the pack. Most people didn't know that Dustin wasn't a clan member anymore and that he now lived here. Their father had been ashamed, and he'd made Mark promise to keep the secret. There was no way the mages would have known about the pack, but they might have sent Lester to spy on the clan.

Mark almost snorted. There didn't seem to be a clan anymore. Dustin hadn't told him much, but he'd explained that many people had died during the attack. Mark had wanted to go there straight away, and Lester had needed to knock him out with the spell to ensure he wouldn't hurt himself again.

Mark didn't want to find out what happened to the clan anymore. He should, but he feared what he'd find. He didn't want to be the alpha, and he didn't want to continue obeying his father's orders, but it was his duty to check in on what remained of the clan and ensure that the people there had what they needed to survive. He couldn't continue hiding in this bedroom, no matter how much he wanted to.

"Mark?" Lester asked.

Mark smiled at him. "I'm fine."

"Are you sure?"

The door slammed open, and Dustin burst in. His expression was frantic, and Mark wondered what had happened. He calmed down when he saw Mark, and Mark realized that his brother had been afraid for him.

Mark had never thought he'd get this. Things between him

and Dustin had changed as they'd grown up, and he'd believed the kind of relationship they'd had when they were kids was forever gone. But Dustin was here for him now. He didn't spend as much time with Mark as Lester, but he was always there when Mark needed him.

"I'm fine," Mark told the two men before they could freak out. They both tended to do that.

"Are you sure?" Lester asked. "You were kind of absent just now. Maybe I should check you over or ask a healer to come."

Mark shook his head and sat up straighter. He almost didn't feel any pain when he did that anymore. "I was just thinking. I'm fine, and I don't need either of you to rush off to get the healer. If I need anything healed, you can do it, Lester."

But things weren't that simple. Lester took a step back, but Dustin didn't. He'd been fussing over Mark since the first time Mark had woken up in this bedroom, and it didn't look like his mother-hen behavior was going to end anytime soon.

He moved to the bed and straightened the blankets even though Mark was under them. He gestured at the dresser once he was happy with how they looked. Mark noticed the tray there and smiled, knowing his brother had thought of him and had decided to bring him food.

"Breakfast?" he asked.

"Yeah."

It took a few moments to get everything situated, and Mark could feel his brother staring at him. Dustin had always been closed off, and asking him what he was thinking never worked, so Mark gave him time.

"You look more awake," Dustin said eventually.

Mark had been chewing on a piece of bacon, so he quickly swallowed. "I *feel* more awake." As far as he could remember, he hadn't been able to spend more than ten minutes without feeling sleepy again since he'd arrived. He felt stronger today, though.

He turned to Lester. "Did you heal me again while I was sleeping?"

Lester's cheeks flushed. "I did. I know you want to be back on your feet as soon as possible."

Mark did but also dreaded the day he'd be allowed out of his bedroom. What would he do? Would he go back to the clan? Would he be offered a place with the pack? If he was, what would his role be?

He had many questions and doubts, and every single one of them terrified him. It was much easier to stay in this bedroom, protected from what was happening outside its door.

"Once you are, you'll be able to start a new life," Dustin said, smiling. "Lester, too. He can leave and do whatever he wants now that he's free from the coven."

Mark panicked. He didn't want Lester to leave. He probably shouldn't want him to stay, but he couldn't imagine not having Lester by his side. They'd been through a lot together, and Lester had protected Mark. He'd been Mark's only human contact while he was locked up with the coven, and the thought of not having him anymore made him want to beg Lester not to leave.

Instead, he swallowed another piece of bacon. Did he belong with the pack? Did Lester? Was Lester actually as good as he appeared to be? Maybe he was, and maybe he wasn't. Only time would tell if Lester was honest or if he'd been sent to spy on the pack.

Mark hoped he hadn't been. He didn't want Lester to be one of the bad guys.

And he didn't want to let him go.

Lester liked that Dustin was so positive about his future, but he didn't feel the same way. He might be free from the coven, but what about the pack? And if the pack made him leave, what was he supposed to do?

He was alone, and he'd never been alone before. He didn't know how to get a job or find a home. He didn't know anything because the coven had ensured he didn't. They'd kept him in the dark when it came to surviving on his own, and it felt like they might have won.

"I don't want Lester to go," Mark said.

From his expression, he was as surprised as Lester by his words. Lester didn't know what to think of it, but it gave him a reason to stick around, which was what he'd hoped for.

"I'll stay, then," he said. "At least until you're healed." Lester was pretty sure James would pitch a fit if he was allowed to stay longer than that, and he didn't want to push his luck. He could stay until Mark was better, though. He'd make sure Mark was fully healed before leaving.

It was hard to imagine a life without the coven. Unless someone helped him, Lester was pretty sure he'd end up on the streets. He didn't want to return to the coven, but he felt he might not have a choice. That was why he was happy to let Mark dictate when he could leave. This place might feel like a prison the same way the coven had, but it was a prison that fed and housed him and didn't hurt him.

He didn't like feeling like he was taking advantage, but he didn't feel he had a choice. It was either this or ending up on the streets immediately, and he had no idea how to deal with that. He might not want to return to the coven, but he couldn't help but wonder if he'd eventually feel he didn't have a choice.

They would hurt him and punish him, and he'd probably regret returning, but he was sure they'd eventually take him back in because they'd never waste magical power. They'd treat him barely better than how they treated the dragons, but at least he'd have a roof over his head and people around him. He might even get his friends back.

"Don't even think about it," Dustin snapped.

It took Lester a second to realize he was talking to him. "Don't even think about what?"

"I've already been through everything you're going through now. I know how desperate you feel. Without your coven, you don't have anything. You don't know how to survive. Do you know how many times I almost went back to my father? I was homeless for a long time and alone for most of it. I didn't feel I could continue surviving like that."

"How did you resist the urge to go back?" That was what Lester needed to know.

"I met people. You know Theo, right?"

"He and Chance visited a few days ago," Lester confirmed.

"He and his brother were homeless for a while, too. Eventually, a bunch of us gathered, and we became a family. The pack can be that for you, Lester. You don't have to go if you don't want to. You'll be allowed to stay for as long as you want."

Lester wanted to believe him, but he didn't make the decisions. Alpha Chance did, and his closest advisors helped him. Houston might be on Lester's side because Dustin was, but there was no way James would want Lester to stay.

He hadn't attacked Lester or anything like that, but he'd been vocal about his feelings. Lester suspected he'd wanted to kick him out as soon as they were back in pack territory, but Dustin had begged for Lester to be allowed to stay with Mark. He'd pointed out that Lester was the only one who knew what had been done to Mark.

Mark wouldn't need him forever.

He didn't know much about the pack, but he'd seen enough to make him want to stay. The people here seemed to really care about each other. They even cared about Mark, even though they didn't know him. He mattered to Dustin, and Dustin was one of theirs. That was why Mark had been welcomed with open arms. Lester was here because of him, and no matter what Dustin said, he wasn't sure he'd be welcome to stay.

He should talk to Chance, but he was afraid. What if Chance confirmed the fact that Lester wasn't welcome? What if he told him he needed to leave right away? Lester wouldn't have anything to pack. Dustin had given him several changes of clothes and toiletries, but that was all he had, and they didn't feel like they were his.

He was twenty-six, and he had nothing. He only had his magic, but he doubted it would help him out there in the world. He couldn't make money out of thin air. He couldn't make a house appear.

But it was time to start thinking about what the future would bring. With Mark getting better, Lester couldn't avoid it anymore.

"I'm going to get you more food," Dustin said as he took the tray from Mark.

Mark blinked down, looking almost surprised that his plate was empty. Lester was, too, but it was good. Mark was finally eating the way he should, which meant he'd recuperate much faster.

That meant Lester had to make things right.

He waited until Dustin was gone to turn to Mark. He felt stiff in a way he never had with Mark, but this situation felt awkward. "I wanted to apologize to you."

Mark frowned. "What for? Did something happen while I was sleeping?"

"No. I'm apologizing for what my coven did. They attacked and destroyed your clan. They hurt you and countless other people. They did all of that because they want power, and it's not right. I'm sorry I was ever part of the coven, and if I could, I'd fix everything they did."

"You told me you weren't there during the attack," Mark said.

"I wasn't. My coven wouldn't trust me to be there. They know I'm softhearted."

"I'd say that more than softhearted, you have morals. You don't care about your own power and what could make it grow. You certainly wouldn't attack a clan of dragons just to become stronger."

Lester swallowed. "I would never do anything to make myself stronger. I don't care about my magic." He only cared about it because it might mean he'd be able to survive out there on his own, but he didn't need more power or money or anything like that. He just wanted enough not to have to worry about where his next meal would come from.

"I don't hold you responsible for what they did, and I don't think anyone should."

"But I could have tried to stop them. I could have freed you sooner and done more to free the other dragons."

Lester didn't want to think about them because there was nothing he could do for them. It broke his heart, but he reminded himself that he'd saved Mark and Wade. It might not feel like enough, but it was better than nothing. It would have been much easier for him to turn the other way and ignore what the coven was doing, but he'd finally been brave enough to stand up to them.

He didn't know if it would be enough, but he wouldn't have been able to live with himself if he'd done nothing. He had no idea what it meant for his future beyond the fact that he was away from the coven for the first time in his life and had opportunities he never would have had if he'd stayed.

He'd change his life in a way he'd never thought he could, and he was proud of himself for that. No matter what happened next, he could never forget that.

The expression on Lester's face broke Mark's heart, no matter how many times he told himself that technically, Lester was the enemy.

Was he, really? Mark would have said yes when he'd first met Lester, but he'd quickly changed his mind about the mage. Lester was the only one who had tried to protect him when he'd been with the mages, and even now that it would have been easier and better for him to leave, he was still here. He stood by Mark's side and protected and healed him, even though he had no obligation to do so.

What was Mark supposed to do? He had no idea what was happening in his own life, yet here he was, yearning to protect a man who should be his enemy.

But it was easy to forget that Lester was a member of the coven that had attacked the clan. They had a lot in common. They'd both been born into a powerful group led by a powerful leader. They'd both been forced to do what that leader expected them to, and neither of them had ever had a say about their life or their future.

Now, they did.

Dustin had mentioned what had happened to the clan without going into details. With so many members dead or moving away to find safety, there wasn't a clan anymore. That was why Mark's father had refused to help get him back. He'd felt he didn't need an heir now that he didn't have a clan.

If Mark had ever wondered if his father cared about him, he knew the truth now. Luckily for him, he hadn't expected his father to care. He hadn't been surprised that he wouldn't be coming for him, but he felt guilty even though he was glad that his father was out of his life.

What about everyone else? What about the dragons who couldn't afford to move or those who'd lost someone? Mark didn't even know who had died and who had survived. He was desperate to know if his friends were all right, but at the same time, he was terrified. What if Rex or Charles had died? What if Mark had lost them?

He didn't know what he'd do and didn't want to find out. He wanted to hide and ignore the rest of the world for just a few more days. He wouldn't be able to do that for much longer. He was almost fully healed, and he'd have to start making decisions when he was.

First, he needed to take care of Lester. Lester felt guilty about what his coven had done, which was understandable, but he shouldn't feel that way if he wasn't a spy for them.

"What would have happened if you'd tried to stop them?" Mark asked.

Lester raised a hand to his face. His fingertips skimmed his scar before he grimaced and dropped his hand.

"They would have hurt me," he murmured.

"So the only thing that would have happened would have been that you'd have been hurt, and they still would have attacked the clan, right?"

"Logically, I know that I'm only one man and couldn't have done anything, but it's hard to accept. It feels like I should have done more."

Mark settled deeper against the pillows behind his back. He was already tiring, which didn't make sense since he'd only been awake half an hour and was doing nothing with his days but sleep. "I should have done more when the coven attacked. I should have defended my clan harder. If I had, there would be more survivors."

"That's not true. If you'd fought harder, the coven would have killed you like they killed the others."

Marcus stared at Lester and waited for him to get it. When he did, he glared, which made Mark smile.

"Now you understand," he gently teased. "There's only

one of you, and your coven is powerful. We both know what would have happened if you'd tried stopping them from attacking the clan. Even if they didn't kill you, they would have hurt you, and if they had, I wouldn't be here today. You didn't know it at the time, but you saved my life by staying back."

"I just don't understand how you can stand to look at me knowing I could have done more."

Mark wasn't sure. He should be angry at Lester for being a mage and keeping him prisoner instead of letting him go the first day he got there.

But what would have happened if he had? Mark hadn't been able to walk back then, and he certainly wouldn't have been able to defend himself if the coven had found him escaping. Lester had kept him safe, and he was the only reason Mark had made it out of there alive.

He rubbed his face. "I think it's because we're similar. Your coven attacked my clan, but I can easily imagine my clan attacking your coven. It's the kind of thing my father would have done, and if he had, I would have been in your place. I wouldn't have been allowed to protest, and if I had, I would have paid for it. You shouldn't be so hard on yourself, Lester. You did everything you could with what you had."

And he'd lost everything by doing so. Unless he was a spy, he'd lost the only place he'd ever called home and the people he'd called family. Even if his parents weren't good people, he had to have had friends. Mark had heard him mention a few people. If Lester had anyone, he'd have to abandon them. They might be in danger because of what he'd done, yet he'd been ready to sacrifice them to help and do what he thought was right.

Mark looked down at his hands. "Both of us are also in a similar place in our life. We lost everything and are confused about what the future will be like. I don't know about you, but I have no idea where I am mentally. Before the attack, I was my father's heir. I had my entire life planned for me. I was going to marry the woman my father chose for me and create an alliance with another clan. I might have had children, and I would have guided the clan when my father died. All of that is gone, and I don't know what I'll do."

"You can do whatever you want."

Mark looked up. "What if I don't know what I want? I was never allowed to have dreams. I always knew the clan was the only thing I'd ever have. It was pointless to dream."

And now, Mark had no idea where he stood.

It was terrifying.

A knock on the door interrupted them. Mark was grateful because he was done with this conversation. He wasn't even thinking about it anymore. He'd find out what he'd do in the future when the future arrived. For now, he was happy to hide in the present.

"Yes?" Lester called out.

The door opened. Mark was only half surprised to see Theo, the alpha mate, peek in. He smiled when he saw Mark awake and stepped inside, quickly followed by the alpha.

"It's good to see you awake," Chance said.

"I'm not sure it's good to be awake, but I'm dealing with it," Mark told him.

There was understanding and compassion in Chance's eyes. Maybe he understood what Mark was going through, but even if he didn't, he could tell how hard it was.

"Since both of you are here, Theo and I wanted to see you," Chance said. "I'll be quick so I don't tire you out, Mark. After a lot of thinking and talking, Theo and I agree that both of you are welcome to stay with the pack."

"For how long?" Lester asked.

Chance turned to him. "For as long as you'd like. You're welcome to become pack members."

Mark had expected something like this to happen. Lester

clearly hadn't, though, because his mouth dropped open as he stared at Chance.

"But why? I'm your enemy," he said.

"Are you really?" Chance asked. "Because it looks like you saved two of my people."

"I did the only thing I could. It doesn't mean you should welcome me into your pack. How can you trust me?"

"Trust is something that's built, so you're right, I probably shouldn't trust you. I'm choosing to do so. I don't think you'll break that trust, but if you do, I'll deal with the consequences of my decision."

Mark didn't think Lester would, either, and he was glad to see he wasn't the only one. Lester had been desperate for a place to call home and might have just found it.

Apparently, so had Mark.

Chapter Five

"Where are you taking me?" Lester asked Dustin.

He looked back at the door to Mark's room. He should be in there, keeping an eye on him, even though Mark didn't need him anymore. He'd healed, and while his body still needed time to fully recover, he could finally leave the house and get on with his life.

Lester had no idea what would come next for him, but he'd decided not to think about it unless he absolutely had to. For now, it was better to wonder what was happening. Dustin knew Lester felt uncomfortable with anyone who wasn't Mark, yet he'd still come to drag him off. That had to mean he had something planned, but what?

Should Lester be afraid?

Dustin's smile told him he shouldn't. He'd only met Dustin recently, but they were somewhat friends, and Lester didn't think Dustin would hurt him even if he had the opportunity to do so. Not only was Lester taking care of his brother, but Dustin didn't seem like the kind of guy who would hurt anyone, even though he was grumpy often. Dustin's boyfriend had told Lester that under that grumpiness, there was a happy guy who didn't know how to deal with feelings, and Lester believed him. Houston knew Dustin better than anyone, possibly even better than Mark.

"It's a surprise," Dustin said.

"Surprises are never good when they happen to me. Did I do something wrong?" Was Dustin kicking Lester out?

Dustin stopped moving as they reached the stairs. "You

didn't do anything wrong," he reassured Lester. "You've been incredible since you arrived here, and I don't know what I would have done without you. I don't want you to worry about this kind of thing."

"I wasn't worried until you dragged me away from Mark."

Dustin stared at Lester for a moment. Lester wondered what he was looking for and whether he found it. He didn't know, because Dustin didn't mention anything. Instead, his smile widened. "You spent a lot of time with my brother lately."

"Because he needs help."

"He did initially, but not anymore. He's up and moving around, and even though he's still spending a lot of time in bed, he's healed. That's all thanks to you, so don't worry about me doing anything. But you have to see that Mark doesn't need you anymore."

Dustin was right. Mark didn't need Lester, and it didn't matter that Lester wanted to feel needed. Mark was ready to return to a normal life, which might not include Lester.

He still hadn't made his decision. He desperately wanted to stay with the pack, but it wouldn't be easy. He'd never lived with shifters, and they didn't trust him. He didn't know if he trusted them, either. He trusted people like Dustin, Wade, and even the alpha, but almost everyone else kept staring at him like he was a bug on the ground, and he didn't like that.

He'd never treated anyone that way, and he'd never cared about what someone was. He didn't believe shifters were bad people or animals, just like he didn't believe that mages were better than everyone else. If anything, his experience had shown him that wasn't the case. Mages could be just as cruel as shifters, if not more.

"That doesn't mean anyone expects you to leave," Dustin said gently. "In fact, I'm pretty sure Mark doesn't want you out of his sight."

Lester frowned. "Why not? Does he think I'll betray him and the pack if I'm not with him?"

Dustin patted Lester's shoulder. "You don't see it yet, but you will soon. Come on. The surprise is waiting."

Lester allowed Dustin to guide him downstairs. He was still thinking about what Dustin had said, but he couldn't make sense of it, not even when Dustin started talking again.

"You know, our father arranged a marriage both for me and my brother. I knew I couldn't go through with it, but also that I wasn't the only one. I don't think Mark would have gotten married if it had come to it. Maybe if our father had chosen a man for him, but a woman? There's no way."

Lester wondered if he'd heard that right. Was Dustin really saying what he thought Dustin was saying? But why would he want Lester to know that his brother was gay? Lester was too afraid to ask, so he was glad when they walked into the living room to find a bunch of people waiting for them. Lester's first instinct was to turn around and return upstairs, but Dustin grabbed his arm and pulled him toward the group.

Lester relaxed when he saw that Wade was there. Wade waved at him and patted the space next to him on the couch, which meant he wanted Lester close. Lester didn't understand why, but he wasn't going to argue. Wade was one of the few people who were nice to him.

Apart from Wade, Dustin, and Theo, Lester didn't know any of the other people here. It made him nervous.

"We thought we could have some fun this afternoon and watch a movie together," Wade explained. "You already know Dustin and Theo, and these are all members of our small ragtag pack." He leaned closer and bumped his shoulder against Lester's. "Don't tell James, but I still consider these guys my pack more than I do the bears, even though we've been here for a while. The bonds we forged on the streets just aren't the same as those we now have with the pack."

"I won't tell him," Lester assured him because he never spoke to James if he could avoid it.

Wade beamed. "Well, this is Seth, Theo's brother. Then we have Thomas, Matty, Josie, and Paisley. Not everyone could make it, but you'll meet the others soon."

He indicated the people he introduced one at a time, and Lester waved at them like an idiot. They didn't seem to care. They either waved back or smiled at him, and he took his time watching their reaction. They were comfortable and settled in for an afternoon of fun.

He hadn't expected it and certainly hadn't expected to be included. He wasn't sure what to think of it, but he knew how it made him feel.

It felt great because it meant he was accepted, but at the same time, it hurt because it reminded him of the friends he'd left back home.

He hadn't reached out to them and didn't think he should. If they weren't already in trouble with the coven, he didn't want them to be, and he certainly didn't want to bring trouble to the pack. Had the elders interrogated his friends to find out what they knew about what had happened and where Lester was? They might be hurting them right now to get answers. His friends might even be dead, although Lester told himself that the elders wouldn't do something like that.

"I thought you'd want to watch a movie, but maybe it's not your thing," Wade said slowly.

Lester realized his expression must have made him think he wasn't happy. "It's not that. I'm fine watching a movie, but it reminds me of when I did it with my friends."

"You had to leave them behind."

Wade's tone was understanding and almost made Lester cry. "I did. They were too scared to help with Mark, and I don't blame them. I was lucky that everything was all right in the end, but it also might not have been. I just wish I could find out how they are."

Wade wiggled and reached into his pocket, taking out a phone. He held it out to Lester, who blinked at it. Wade's expression was set. "They won't associate my number with you, but if they do, we'll deal with it. It'll be fine. Call your friends and see how they are. You won't be able to relax otherwise."

He was right. Lester looked around the room at the people gathered there. The TV was on, and they were all sitting on the couches and armchairs, or even on the floor, where Seth looked comfortable. They weren't watching Lester or expecting him to start hurting them. They just wanted him to be part of their group, and he felt welcome in a way he hadn't in a long time.

He wanted Cole, Chris, and Hannah to feel the same way. He wanted them to be safe and to know that nothing would happen to them.

He wanted time with them.

He still wasn't sure this was a good idea, but he took Wade's phone anyway. His fingers shook as he dialed Chris's number. He'd had to leave his phone behind, but he remembered Chris's number.

"Hello?" Chris asked when he answered.

He sounded curious, which made sense since he wouldn't recognize the number. "Chris?"

Chris sucked in a breath. "Lester?"

Lester smiled. "Yeah, it's me."

Mark stared at the phone Dustin had given him. It was time to call his father and find out what was happening, but he didn't want to.

He wanted to act like a child and hide under the blankets. So far, he'd been allowed to do that, but time was up. He was healed thanks to Lester, and it didn't hurt when he moved anymore. His body still felt weak sometimes, but Lester had assured him it would pass soon. He'd lost blood and had a punctured lung, and even though Lester had used magic to heal him, his body would need some time to recuperate fully. Lester had ordered Mark to take things slow, and Mark had been more than happy to obey.

But being healed meant it was time to stop hiding and find out what had happened the night of the attack and since then. Dustin hadn't been able to give Mark many details. Their father had refused to talk to him except once when he'd told Dustin that he didn't have a clan anymore, so he didn't need an heir. He'd thought Mark was dead and hadn't planned to look for him. He didn't care enough.

Mark had always suspected that, but it hurt to have it confirmed. Even though he'd known his father didn't care, part of him still yearned for his love and approval. Now that it was confirmed that he would never get it, Mark didn't want to talk to his father again. That part of his life was behind him, and he was happy about that.

But even though he wasn't his father's heir anymore, he still felt responsible for the clan. If there was anything he could do for any of them, he wanted to do it. The only way to find out was to call his father, so after staring at the phone for what felt like forever, he finally pulled up the number he needed and pressed call.

"What?" his father snapped when he answered.

That was how he always answered the phone, so Mark wasn't surprised or offended. "Dad? It's me, Mark."

There was a moment of what Mark imagined was a shocked silence. If his father had thought he was dead, he wouldn't have expected him to call. Would this change anything? Would Mark's father ask him to return and change his mind about the pack? They might have lost a lot of members, but it didn't mean they didn't need an alpha anymore.

"You're alive," Mark's father said.

He didn't sound happy about it, but he also didn't sound angry, which Mark supposed was positive.

"I am. I managed to escape from where the coven held me. It took some time to heal from my wounds, but I'm fine now." Mark's father would never ask him how he was or how he felt.

"There's no reason for you to come back, so you should stay where you are."

Mark had known that, but it still knocked his breath out. "You don't want me to come home? I'm fine now. I can come back and get to work. We can rebuild the clan."

There was nothing Mark wanted less. He didn't want to be an alpha and didn't think his father should be one, either, but it was all Mark knew. If he wasn't his father's successor, what was he? *Who* was he?

He'd never been allowed to be anyone else, and at thirty-six, it left him feeling lost. He was glad Chance had offered him a place with the pack, but he wasn't sure he belonged here.

His father snorted. "Rebuild the clan? There's nothing to rebuild. You'd have to have something left to do that, and I don't. Everyone is gone, including you."

Mark had known it was terrible, but surely his father was exaggerating. "I know many people died and some left, but there has to be someone who stayed."

"Not really. There are a few families, but I've heard they've been considering leaving, too. They have too many bad memories." Mark's father snorted again. "I might leave, too. There's a new pack in the area, and they contacted me about the land. I'm going to sell it to them."

Mark didn't know what to say. For most of his life, he'd wanted to escape. He'd never wanted to become the alpha after his father and to be in charge of the clan and the land, but now that his father was taking both of them from him, he wanted to argue it wasn't fair. This was what he'd wanted, so why wasn't he happy?

Could he ever be happy again?

He told himself not to be dramatic. No matter what happened, he had people who cared about him. Dustin was happy to have him here, and he'd told him he could stay in the house for as long as he wanted. He'd said he wanted to fix their relationship, and Mark wanted the same. It would be impossible if he went back to the clan, and his father told him he didn't have to.

"What about the clan members who are still there?" he asked. "What will you do about them?"

"We're not a clan anymore, so what they do doesn't matter. They can go or stay. I don't care."

"You were their alpha for decades. How can you not care?"

"I lost my clan," Mark's father snapped. "What do you want me to do? We have no allies left. We have nothing. You'll never be an alpha, and you should focus on turning your life around. I know you're with your brother, so you shouldn't have a problem doing that. He's with those wolves."

Mark almost rolled his eyes. "Bears."

"Whatever. I don't care who your brother is fucking. He hasn't been a clan member in a long time, and you're not one anymore, either. There's no clan. Make your peace with that and let it go."

"We still have a duty to the survivors."

"You might feel like you do, but I don't. I gave the clan my everything, and it wasn't enough. I'm not doing that again."

That didn't sound like Mark's father, but Mark didn't know what to do about it. He wasn't even sure there *was* anything he could do about it.

His father hung up before Mark could add anything. Mark stared at the phone.

He wasn't surprised there wasn't much left of the clan. Dustin had warned him, and even though it had sounded impossible, Mark hadn't believed him. The mages were strong and had used magic to make the dragons unable to shift. Without being able to shift, they had no way to defend themselves.

But it still hurt. It felt like a huge part of Mark's life was gone, and he didn't know how to go on without it. He didn't know what he was supposed to do now or what was expected of him.

He'd never been free to decide what he wanted to do with his life. He'd never been allowed to dream or make any decisions. The only thing he'd ever done was spend time with his father and watch him be an alpha. He'd always felt it was ridiculous because he couldn't learn anything by watching his father yell at people, but he'd gone through with it because it was what was expected of him.

None of that mattered anymore.

He swallowed and put his phone down. He knew what had happened to the clan now, but he still had no idea if his friends were alive. He wanted to ask his father, but he'd also been afraid of the answer. What had happened to Charles and Rex? Were they looking for him? Or had Mark's father told them he was dead?

Either he hadn't, or they were dead, because if they knew he was here, they would have already knocked on his door. Knowing that made Mark want to cry and scream.

It wasn't fair. The mages had taken everything from him, and he wanted them to pay. He wanted to find the coven house, burn it to the ground, and stomp out any mage escaping from the burning building. He wanted to tear off limbs and heads and to revel in the pain and horror he created.

It wasn't like him, but he didn't care right now.

After all, he didn't know who he was beyond being his father's heir. Maybe he was a monster.

Maybe he would wipe out the coven.

Lester was supposed to stay downstairs with the others and watch the movie, but when he'd realized the conversation with Chris would be heavy, he'd excused himself. Wade had waved him away when he'd explained he needed his phone for a bit longer, which Lester hoped meant he didn't need it back soon.

"The coven is a mess," Chris said. "We still have a few dragons, but the coven killed a lot of them in the attack, and the elders were counting on your dragon. The fact that you took him away has everyone pissed, and they've branded you a traitor."

Lester swallowed. Being branded a traitor meant that the coven would be hunting him. They would capture and drag him back to the coven house if they found him. Once there, they'd torture him until they were satisfied, which usually meant they would do so until he died.

He'd known all of that before leaving, yet he'd still left. He couldn't regret his actions, no matter how often he told himself everything would have been fine if he'd ignored Mark's pain.

How could he have? How could he have ignored what the coven had done and the many people they'd killed? If this was what they did when they went on missions, Lester didn't want anything to do with them. He was done with the coven, even if it meant his death.

He hoped it wouldn't. He still had many years to live, and now that he was free, he wanted to enjoy those years. The problem was that he wouldn't be able to if the coven was after him.

He was putting everyone here in danger. Eventually, the coven would find him, and when they did, they would attack the pack. They would destroy it like they'd destroyed Mark's clan, and Lester couldn't do anything about it because he was only one man. What could he do against dozens of mages with more training and experience than him?

"Please tell me you're safe," Chris said. "I didn't know what to think when I found out you were gone. The elders talked to me and the others, but we didn't know anything, so they let it go. Is that why you didn't tell us you were leaving?"

"I didn't tell you because I wasn't planning on doing anything. It was a spur-of-the-moment decision." One Lester hadn't made.

That had been Wade, and even though Lester had been convinced they'd be found and killed, Wade had been right. They'd managed to sneak out of the house and leave in one piece. A lot of that was thanks to Wade and James, so Lester could never hate James, no matter how much he scared him.

"But you're safe?"

Lester stopped in the hallway and leaned against the wall. He'd stopped in front of the window so he could look outside. He needed the sight of the trees and the peacefulness of the woods that surrounded pack territory.

He took a deep breath. "I am. You don't have to worry about me."

"How can I not? The coven is going to find you."

That was what Lester was afraid of. "I know they will eventually, but I'm not alone. Maybe we'll find a way to push them back."

"Push them back? That's not possible, Lester. The coven is too strong. I'd tell you to come back and beg for mercy, but I don't think it would change anything. Right now, you're safer away from us than you are with us."

Chris didn't know how right he was. Lester wanted to protect the pack, and the pack wanted to protect him. It didn't feel right, but that was the truth. Mark would stand up for him. Dustin and Wade would, too. Chance and Theo, Houston, and a bunch of other people would help. It might mean their death, but they wouldn't abandon Lester.

This was nothing like the coven. That was why Lester wanted to stay, even though he shouldn't. He was putting the pack in danger, but he couldn't find it in himself to leave. He didn't want to be alone.

"You could come," Lester said before he could think better of it.

"What are you talking about?"

"I left with the dragon shifter, and his brother brought us to his pack. We've been staying here, and the alpha has offered me a permanent place with them. I'm sure that if I ask, he'd welcome you and the others, just like he welcomed me."

"You want Hannah, Cole, and me to join you?"

"Yes. You know that what they're doing isn't right. They're hurting people and killing them, and they're not doing it to defend themselves or the coven. They're doing it because they want power."

"We can't leave. I'm not as strong as you, Lester. What would I do?"

"Whatever you want. I don't know what I'll do, either, but at least now, I have a chance to find out. I have people who care about me and will protect me if the coven finds me, and you can have the same. You can have freedom."

It was something they'd often talked about. None of them had believed they could ever have it, but it had felt good to dream.

Now, they *could* have it. Lester had offered it to his best friend, hoping Chris would take the opportunity. He'd understand if he didn't, but he wasn't willing to abandon his friends.

"How can we trust that pack?" Chris asked.

"I know it's hard, but this is a leap of faith. You have to decide you want to trust them and see what happens."

"I don't know, Lester. I'll talk to the others, but I can't make promises. You know what our life is like. We don't have anything outside of the coven."

"I'm offering you something. Just think about it, all right? You don't have to give me an answer right away."

"Yeah, all right. I'll call you soon."

Lester didn't want him to hang up, but he let Chris go. He had to.

He put the phone in his pocket and wondered if he should go back downstairs. Wade would expect him to, as would Dustin, but he didn't think he could. He needed a moment to himself so he could wrap his mind around what had just happened.

He decided to check on Mark. When he was with him, he felt normal and could forget the mess his life was. He was already upstairs, anyway. Maybe he could convince Mark to come downstairs and watch the movie with him and the others.

He knocked on the bedroom door as soon as he reached it, waited for Mark's answer, then opened it. Mark was on the bed like Lester had expected, but his expression told Lester something was wrong.

"What is it?" he asked, rushing to Mark's side. "Are you hurt?"

Mark shook his head. "I called my father."

Lester knew that Mark hadn't expected the call with his father to go well, and it obviously hadn't. Lester understood how Mark felt. Even though he'd known the call with Chris would be hard, he'd still hoped that maybe the coven had finally realized what they were doing wasn't right or maybe his friends would be brave enough to join him.

They hadn't. It had gone exactly how Lester had expected, and he was disappointed.

Not as disappointed as Mark. Even though he'd known his father would brush him off, the man was still his father. Lester didn't have much affection for his parents, but he often wondered what it would have been like to have loving parents who wanted the best for him.

He moved toward the bed before he could think about it. Since he'd met Mark, the only thing he'd ever wanted was to help and support him. He wanted to comfort him and wipe the sadness from his expression, even though he didn't know how to do it.

He sat beside Mark, who looked startled but didn't ask him to leave. For a moment, they stayed silent. Lester tried to come up with something he could say that would make Mark feel better.

"He's an asshole," he eventually said.

Mark snorted, then laughed. "That he is."

"I'm sorry he treated you like that, but it's clear he never cared about you." Maybe that wasn't the best thing to say. "What I mean is that you don't need him anymore. You have me and Dustin and Houston and everyone else here."

Mark stared at Lester. "Do I?"

"Do you what?"

"Have you?"

Lester had thought it was obvious. "Of course you do. You know what I sacrificed for you. You know what I did because I couldn't stand to see you hurt."

"Wouldn't you have done that for anyone?"

Lester shook his head. "I had the opportunity to help others. The clan weren't the first people the coven attacked, and while I always thought it was wrong and horrible, I never did anything to stop them or to help some of the people they grabbed. You were the first."

Lester always tried to be honest with Mark. He didn't want to lie to him because he cared about him.

He hadn't expected Mark's reaction to his words. For a moment, neither of them moved. That didn't last long. Mark reached for Lester, and Lester sucked in a breath as the dragon shifter pulled him into his arms. He hadn't known he wanted this, but as soon as Mark's lips landed on his, he was sure of it.

This was where he was supposed to be—with this pack and in Mark's arms.

This had been a long time coming. Mark wouldn't lie to himself. He'd been attracted to Lester since the first time he'd seen him, but it had been easy to ignore it between the pain, barely being conscious, and knowing that Lester was technically an enemy.

Not anymore. Unless Lester was a phenomenal actor, there was no way he was here to spy on the pack or Mark. No one would be able to keep up the pretense as well as he had and for so long. Mark was sure he could trust Lester.

He prayed he wasn't wrong.

He'd lost it when Lester had said he was there for him. Mark knew Lester wasn't going anywhere, but it was different to hear it. Lester could have left Mark behind so many times, but he hadn't. He'd been there for him, just like he'd said, since Mark had woken up in the coven house in pain and not knowing where he was. If it wasn't for Lester, Mark would be dead or close to it. He didn't know what Lester had seen in him and didn't care as long as Lester stayed with him.

Mark hadn't been sure Lester felt the same way. Sometimes, he wondered if Lester spent so much time with him because he felt guilty. He was a mage, so even though he didn't have anything to do with what his coven had done, it would make sense for him to feel guilty and want to make it up to Mark. It didn't matter how many times Mark told him he didn't need to.

But Mark had hoped there was more to it, and now that he had Lester in his arms, he was sure he'd been right. Lester didn't push him away. He didn't tell him this was a mistake and that he only liked him as a friend. Instead, he snuggled deeper in Mark's embrace, one of his arms going around Mark's waist as he turned his upper body to move closer. Sitting side by side on the bed wasn't the most comfortable position to kiss, but Lester didn't seem to care, and they made it work without ever stopping.

Lester's lips were soft. He moved hesitantly as if he didn't quite know what to do. Mark wouldn't have been surprised if he didn't. From what Lester had told him, he'd been sheltered, but not because his parents wanted to protect him. He hadn't been allowed to experience the world around him, and this might even be his first kiss.

Mark didn't care if it was. He just wanted to feel Lester against him, and he had him. It felt so damn good that he had to resist the urge to pull Lester into his lap. That would probably be too much for a first kiss, especially with someone as inexperienced as Lester.

He was gentle and sweet and deserved to be protected. If Lester's parents wouldn't do it, then Mark would.

"Are you sure we should be doing this?" Lester eventually asked.

Mark frowned. "Why shouldn't we? You don't want it?"

Lester's cheeks were already flushed, but they darkened further. "I want it very much, but it might not be the smartest idea in our situation. We should be enemies."

"Why? Because you're a mage and I'm a dragon? Do you care?"

"Of course not."

"Then I don't see what the problem is. You're a good person, Lester, one of the best I've ever met. I don't care about what you are or what you can do, only about your actions, and you've shown me I can trust you. The circumstances in which we met might not have been the best, but it doesn't mean we shouldn't do this just because of that. The only thing that should stop us is if we don't want it. I do."

He didn't have to ask if Lester wanted it, too. He kissed Mark this time, a soft gasp dying against Mark's mouth. It felt almost frantic, as if Lester feared that Mark would change his mind if he didn't hurry. Mark wanted to tell him nothing could make him change his mind, but he didn't want to stop kissing Lester.

So he didn't.

Both Mark and Lester deserved someone who would love them and want them for who they were and wouldn't try to change them or force them into a box. They deserved someone who would be there for them and comfort them when no one else would.

Mark had Dustin and Houston, but it wasn't the same. As much as Dustin loved Mark, his main focus was Houston, as it should be. Mark wanted someone who would be there just for him, and he thought that maybe he'd found it in Lester.

Realizing that was freeing. Mark had always been afraid he would never have this. He'd expected to have to marry a woman his father had chosen for him, and he'd known how awful it would be for both of them. He'd made his peace with knowing he'd never find love.

He didn't know if what was growing between him and Lester *was* love, but he felt that even if it wasn't yet, it could change. Mark wanted nothing more than to love and be loved, and he didn't care that Lester was a mage. The only important thing was that he was Lester, and he was a delightful man to know and grow to love.

Vibrations pulled Mark out of the kiss. He blinked, wondering if his father was calling, but the screen was dark when he looked down at the phone he'd abandoned in his lap. Lester wiggled until he could take out a phone from his pocket. Mark hadn't realized he had one.

When Lester looked at the screen, he smiled, so it had to be a good thing.

Lester answered, immediately putting the phone on speaker. "Hey, Chris," he said. "Why are you calling back? You've already made your decision? Mark is with me, and I'd like the two of you to meet."

There was a moment of silence. "This is Sophia."

By the way Lester quickly paled, it was clear that whoever this Sophia was, it wasn't a good thing to have her on the phone. Lester had expected one of his friends to be calling, which probably meant Sophia had taken the phone from them. Had she hurt them?

"Where's Chris?" Lester asked. "What have you done to him?"

"He's all right, although no thanks to you. What were you thinking?"

Lester swallowed loudly and turned wide eyes to Mark. Mark wished he could get through the conversation for him, but it was impossible.

"I was thinking that what you did to the dragons is wrong," Lester said. His voice trembled, but only slightly. "You shouldn't kill people just because you want more power. You shouldn't attack them and destroy their lives. You were going to kill Mark, and I couldn't let you do that."

"I always knew your soft heart would ruin you. You lasted longer than I expected, but I'm not surprised you betrayed us. As of right now, I'm banishing you from the coven. You are not one of us anymore. If we see you, we won't have mercy.

Never return if you want to keep your life, Lester, and don't think hiding with your dragon will help you. Eventually, our paths will cross again, and you know who will win when they do."

"Wait! What about Chris? What have you done to him?"

Sophia didn't answer. She'd already hung up. Mark hadn't understood half of what was happening, but he could tell it was bad. He didn't know how to help, so he dragged Lester into his arms.

Lester cried out and dropped the phone. He pressed his face against Mark's neck as if he wanted to hide from the world. If he did, Mark would hold him through it. He'd do everything in his power to make Lester happy, even though it didn't make much sense.

Love seldom did.

Mark didn't care what anyone else thought of him and Lester being together. Lester wanted him. More importantly, he *needed* him, and that was all that mattered.

CHAPTER SIX

"Favorite food?" Lester asked.

Mark sounded convinced when he answered. "Lettuce."

Lester pushed away from Mark's chest and looked down at him. "Lettuce? Really?"

They were both sitting on Mark's bed, getting to know each other. It had started as a playful interrogation on Lester's part, but this was too much. How could anyone's favorite food be *lettuce*?

"What?" Mark asked. "Lettuce is great. It's healthy."

"It doesn't taste of anything. If you don't put dressing on it, it's like eating grass. How can it be your favorite food when chocolate and bacon exist?"

"Is that your favorite food? Chocolate and bacon?"

"Not together, but yeah. They're good."

Lester knew Mark was teasing. He was able to tell from his tone, and it made him feel warm inside.

Mark wanted *him*. He wanted them to be together. Lester suspected his boyfriend didn't fully trust him yet, but that was okay. It made sense, and he wasn't angry at Mark for feeling that way. Considering the circumstances, he would have been surprised if Mark had trusted him from the start.

Mark and Lester had met in weird circumstances. Mark had been in pain and wounded, and Lester was part of the group of people who had hurt him. It was a miracle that Mark had trusted Lester enough to allow him to heal him and get him out of the coven house. Things would have gone so much worse if he hadn't, and Lester was in awe of how strong Mark was. He didn't think a lot of people would have trusted a mage after mages had attacked and killed their people.

Mark had.

Lester playfully pushed Mark. "You're one of those healthy people who only eat vegetables and proteins, aren't you?"

"What else are you supposed to eat? Please tell me you don't eat fast food at every meal."

Lester settled back. "Of course not. The coven wouldn't have allowed me to eat fast food, and it wasn't like I could go out there and get it on my own. I was never allowed to learn to drive, and even if I had been, I wasn't allowed to leave the house much."

Mark wrapped an arm around Lester's shoulders and kissed the top of his head. "I'm sorry. Sometimes, I forget how you grew up."

"It's not your fault."

"But I don't have to remind you of it."

"You didn't remind me on purpose, so it's fine. Besides, the coven is in the past now, isn't it? I'm never going back."

Mark's arm tightened around Lester's shoulders. "Damn right, you aren't. And if they try taking you back, they'll have to fight me."

Lester didn't point out that they already had and that they'd won. He knew all too well that things would end badly if the coven were to attack the pack, but it wasn't something he wanted to think about. He'd be forced to eventually, but he hoped the pack would be better equipped to deal with them when it was time. He'd do everything he could to make sure the pack won.

It might sound weird because the coven had been his family for his entire life, but had they really? More than a family, they'd been people who had forced Lester into a life he'd never wanted. He was glad now that he'd never been allowed to go out on jobs with the other coven members, but it made him wonder if maybe they'd suspected he wouldn't take it well. Was that why they'd kept him away from those jobs? Because they'd known he wouldn't be okay with what they were doing and would try to stop them?

Alone, Lester wouldn't have been able to do anything. He wasn't alone anymore, and he hoped the coven remembered that. They'd strike eventually, but for now, either they didn't know he was with the pack, or they didn't want to attack Chance and his people head-on.

That was perfectly fine with Lester. The less he saw the coven, the better he felt. He hoped he'd never have to think about them again.

But he knew he couldn't just not think about them. His three best friends were still there, and he had no idea what had happened to them. Were they even alive?

The coven didn't usually kill mages. Instead, they humiliated them and kicked them out. Lester had been lucky enough to skip the first part of the usual punishment, but he wasn't welcome there anymore, and that was fine with him. He didn't want to be welcome in a group of people who thought killing innocents was all right.

His phone vibrated on the nightstand. The only people who called him were Wade and his friends, so Lester expected it would be one of them.

He'd told Chance he didn't need a cell phone, but the alpha had insisted. Apparently, now that Lester was a pack member, the pack would make sure he had the basics. That included clothes and a cell phone, which was a relief since Lester had left his behind. He wasn't quite sure what he could do for the pack yet, but he was a mage. There had to be something.

When Lester saw Chance's name on the screen, his mind immediately went to the worst-case scenario. He answered with trembling fingers, hoping he wasn't about to hear that one of the few people he cared about had been hurt—or worse.

"Chance?"

"Hey, Lester. Sorry to bother you."

"You're not bothering me."

"I need to see you right away. Can you come to the house?"

Lester's gaze flicked up to Mark's face. His boyfriend looked worried, maybe because he could feel how tense Lester had gone. "I'm with Mark right now."

"I have no problems if he comes with you. It's nothing bad, so I don't want you to start panicking."

Lester snorted. "I'm *definitely* panicking now."

Chance laughed, which allowed Lester to relax. The alpha wouldn't sound so carefree if whatever was happening was bad.

"We'll be right there," Lester promised.

"We'll be waiting for you."

Lester wanted to ask who Chance meant with that *we*, but if Chance wanted to tell him on the phone, he would have. As soon as they hung up, Lester scrambled out of bed, already looking for his shoes. He found one under the bed, but the other was out of sight, and he needed it.

"Under the chair," Mark said.

Lester located the missing shoe, pulled it on, and turned to his boyfriend. "You're coming with me?"

"You could try keeping me away, but I doubt you'd succeed. Whatever's happening, we'll face it together."

Lester sucked in a breath. He'd known he wasn't alone, but hearing it made his heart feel all tingly. Now wasn't the right moment to push Mark back on the bed, unfortunately, so Lester grabbed his hand and dragged him downstairs.

Luckily, nothing was far in pack territory. Once Lester and Mark had their jackets, it only took a five-minute walk to reach Chance's house. Lester felt like he was about to vibrate out of his skin, but Mark's presence was soothing and helped him keep his calm. It was the only reason he didn't burst into the house demanding to know what was happening.

Theo opened the door when Lester knocked. He smiled at them and even hugged Lester. Lester was a bit surprised when he didn't try talking to them. Instead, he gestured at them to go to Chance's office.

"Everyone is in there."

"Everyone who?" Lester asked.

Theo's eyes widened. "He didn't tell you?"

"Chance didn't tell me anything except that he needed to see me."

"He wanted to surprise you. That's good. At least you'll take it better than James will."

Lester blinked. If James wouldn't take whatever was happening well, it meant it had to do with the pack's safety.

Lester needed to know.

He hung up his jacket and rushed to the office. He didn't check that Mark was coming after him because he already knew his boyfriend was. He burst into the office, knowing he should slow down but unable to do so.

He gaped at the sight in front of him. Like always, Chance was behind his desk, but he wasn't the surprise. The people sitting on the other side of his desk were. The three of them turned when they heard Lester.

The first one out of his seat was Chris. He threw himself at Lester, and it was good that Mark was behind Lester because if he hadn't been, Lester and Chris would have fallen on their asses. Mark grunted when they hit him, but his arms went around Lester briefly, and Lester allowed himself to relax.

Whatever was happening, Mark had him. He wouldn't allow anyone to hurt him, not even the people he considered his best friends.

But Lester wasn't worried that they were here to hurt him. He already knew they weren't.

What he didn't know was *why* they were here exactly.

Mark had no idea who these people were, but from the way Lester was hugging the guy in his arms, it was clear he knew them and cared about them. Mark was surprised the guy's head hadn't popped off from the strength Lester was putting into the hug.

"I think Chris needs to breathe," the second guy said as he rose from the chair where he'd been sitting.

Lester made a wounded sound and turned to the second guy, too. They hugged, although this hug was gentler.

"What are you guys doing here? What happened? Are you hurt?" Lester asked, spilling question after question.

The woman stood up, too. She was the last to hug Lester, and for a moment, Mark wondered if she'd be unable to let go of him. Her eyes were red as if she'd been crying, and she clung to Lester with surprising force.

"What are you doing here?" Lester repeated. "What happened?"

"I'm sure you can imagine my surprise when one of the guards came to me earlier to tell me that three mages wanted to talk to me," Chance said. He was smiling, almost like a proud father.

Mark wanted to ask him what the fuck was going on, but the alpha would tell him as slowly or quickly as he wanted. They'd find out eventually, so Mark wasn't worried as he sat down on the couch, leaving the chairs in front of Chance's desk to Lester's friends.

Lester looked nonplussed. "What? I can't believe that. Did they really let you go?"

The first guy shook his head. "They didn't. We snuck out."

His gaze flickered to Mark. "It's good to see the two of you made it."

Lester beamed. "We did. Mark, these are my three best friends, Chris, Cole, and Hannah. Guys, this is my boyfriend, Mark. He's the dragon shifter I rescued from the coven."

They gaped at Mark, who gave them a little wiggle of his fingers. He felt better now that he knew who they were and was sure he wouldn't have to protect Lester from them.

He supposed the coven might be using them as spies or to get back at Lester, but he didn't think so. These people were Lester's best friends. If they were anything like Lester, they'd rather die than hurt him.

That didn't mean Mark wouldn't keep an eye on them. He wasn't going to stop protecting his boyfriend just because he didn't think his friends would hurt him.

Everyone settled down. Lester sat beside Mark, but he couldn't stop staring at his friends. Mark wanted to tease him, but instead, he knocked their shoulders together, silently telling Lester he was there for him. He wasn't surprised when Lester took his hand and squeezed it.

Lester might never have been in a relationship, but he was very tactile. He liked to be touching Mark, usually holding his hand or leaning against him. It was as if he needed the reassurance that Mark was there for him.

Mark would always be there for him. It would take time for Lester to accept that, but they had time now that they were pack members.

"It figures that you and the dragon ended up together," Chris teased.

Thankfully, he was smiling, so Mark didn't take it badly.

Lester blushed. "It's not like I planned it. Nothing happened between us until recently."

"You saved him," Hannah said quietly. "It would have been much easier for you not to and to continue obeying the elders' orders, but instead, you decided you had enough. You made the right decision, while the three of us didn't."

Mark agreed that Lester was the only one who'd made the right decision, but he didn't blame the three for not helping him. They were only human, and the coven had been their entire life. No matter how bad the elders' decisions had been, it was normal for them to hesitate at the thought of leaving all of it behind and even more so at the risk that one of the people they considered family might kill them.

"What happened?" Lester asked.

His three friends looked at each other. Mark suspected none of them wanted to tell Lester, but they would. They had to if they wanted to stay. There was no way Chance would allow them to stick around if he didn't know the entire truth.

Eventually, Chris sucked in a breath. "We didn't know you'd left. We had lunch and thought we'd see you after that, but your mother found us instead. She asked where you were, but we didn't know. We were confused, especially when she got angry and started yelling."

"That was when the problems started," Hannah interjected. "They dragged the three of us to the elders. We were freaking out because we had no idea what was happening, but you were clearly involved." She paused and briefly closed her eyes. "We thought you'd been hurt or worse. We knew you were spending a lot of time with the dragon, which meant he had to be involved, too, but that was all we were sure of. I think that's what saved us, but at the time, it was terrifying."

"The elders asked us a lot of questions about you," Chris said. "They wanted to know when we'd last seen you and what you were doing in general. We told them that we hadn't seen you since breakfast and that you'd been spending a lot of time with the dragon because your mother had told you to take care of him. I'm not sure how long they interrogated us, but eventually they let us go. I think they realized we truly didn't know anything, even though they'd had doubts initially."

Lester leaned harder against Mark, who wrapped an arm around him. Lester needed his support, and Mark was more than happy to give it to him. This was why they were together, or at least one of the reasons. They were here for each other when they most needed it.

"They left us alone after that," Chris continued. "But we could tell they were watching us. We spent a lot of time together, hiding out in our bedrooms. We wanted to know what had happened to you, but we had no way to find out. We just knew that you and two of the prisoners were gone."

"How did you do it?" Cole asked. "One moment, you were there, and the next, you were gone."

"I met Wade. He was the second prisoner, the one who'd just arrived. The twins were in Mark's bedroom that day, and they ordered me to take care of the new guy. I knew they were going to hurt Mark, but there was nothing I could do about it. I went to Wade, and as soon as I was decently sure he was there to help Mark, I asked him to do just that. Mark had healed enough, and the coven would have started using him soon. I couldn't let that happen. Wade and I dragged Mark out of the house, and I disabled the spells. We were lucky because Wade's boyfriend knew he'd been taken and was looking for him. He and a few other people were outside, and since they'd planned his rescue, they had a van to get us away."

"That's good."

Chris seemed genuinely happy with Lester's explanation, but apparently, Lester wasn't.

"I'm sorry I didn't come to you and ask you to leave with us," Lester said as he leaned forward. "I should have, but there wasn't time. We were lucky that it was lunchtime, but you know how things are at the house. There's always someone around, and we only had that one opportunity."

Mark rubbed a hand on Lester's back. He'd known Lester was missing his friends, and while he wasn't sure what would happen next, it was good to see them together. Hopefully, Chance would realize that the pack would need more mages in case the coven attacked, but Mark wasn't sure they could trust Lester's friends. Lester trusted them with his life, but it was hard not to wonder how they'd made it out of the coven house without as much as a scratch if the coven had really been watching them.

Lester could hardly believe that his friends truly were there. He had so many questions, but he was afraid to find out the answers to most of them. Had they been hurt? What had the elders done to them?

Chris leaned closer. "You have nothing to blame yourself for. You did the only thing you could do to save the dragon, and none of us expected you to come back. Besides, everything is as it should be now, right?"

"If I may ask, how did you escape from the coven?" Chance asked.

"We're not sure, to be honest," Chris said. "After Lester called me, our leader took my phone. It was a matter of minutes, so I'm sure she was spying on me. She called Lester and told him he'd been banished from the coven. I wasn't surprised, but I was freaking out. I thought she was going to do the same to me, but instead, she gave me back my phone and told me to keep in mind what happened to Lester if I didn't want the same to happen to me. I think she believes that being banished from the coven is the worst thing that can happen to a mage, but honestly, as soon as I knew Lester was fine, I couldn't stay. I acted like I was going to and like I didn't care about Lester anymore, and I'm not sure everyone believed me, but I don't think they can comprehend a mage not wanting to be part of the coven."

"Chris came to us," Col quietly. "He told us that Lester had called and everything else, and we knew we had to make a decision. We could stay with the coven and the people we hated or come to Lester."

"How did you find the pack?" Chance asked.

"We use a spell to locate Lester."

Mark sat up straighter, suddenly alarmed. "Mages can do that?"

Lester patted Mark's thigh. "They can, but don't worry. I already blocked the coven from finding me. Chris, Cole, and Hannah used a spell specific to the four of us. That way, we can always find each other, but the rest of the coven can't."

"So we won't suddenly be attacked by the coven?"

Lester grimaced. "I don't know about that. I hope we won't be, but there's no way to know what they'll do."

"I think for now, they're focused on building up power for that spell," Hannah said. "I wouldn't be surprised if they dismissed us. We were never useful to the coven, so it won't be a big loss."

"That's no way to treat pack members," Chance said with a frown.

Hannah shrugged. "The coven never really cared about us. I'm not that powerful, and they always reminded me of that. Lester, Chris, and Cole are different, but for one reason or another, the coven never trusted them. The four of us, along with a bunch of others, were kept away from everything important, so I doubt they'll cry over our disappearance."

"They might still attempt to find us," Chris said. "But we used the same spell as Lester. They won't be able to locate us."

"So you can stay?" Lester asked, turning big eyes to Chance.

Lester wasn't surprised when Chance smiled. He'd

expected it after their short phone conversation.

"I can't say I trust the three of you," the alpha said. "I don't know you, and you'll have to prove that you can earn my trust and the trust of my pack." He looked at Lester's friends. "But like I told Lester, trust is something that's earned, and I'll never be able to trust you if I don't give you a chance to show me that I can. I don't believe you're here to hurt my pack or Lester, so I'll make you the same offer I made him and Mark. You can become pack members. That means protecting the pack, but you'll have to fight by our side if the coven ever attacks. Will you be able to do so? Will you be able to use magic against people you considered family only a few days ago?"

It was a heavy question. Lester had wondered the same thing many times since Chance had made him the offer, and he still wasn't sure that if it came to it, he'd be able to use magic against his mother or father. They might be awful parents, but they were his parents, which would always mean something to him.

He wasn't surprised when his friends were hesitant. The first to nod was Chris, and he did so while looking straight at Chance. "I can't promise I'll be able to kill my parents or siblings, but I can promise to protect the pack with all my ability."

That seemed to be enough for Chance, who nodded back.

Now that Chris had agreed, it seemed easier for the other two to do the same. Cole nodded straight away, and while Hannah was a bit more hesitant, she eventually did the same. Lester could tell they'd expected things to be more complicated, but Chance wasn't that kind of alpha. He was young and down to earth, and for whatever reason, he wanted to trust them. It was hard to understand why, but Lester wasn't about to protest.

"I accept, too," he told Chance. He hadn't given him an answer yet, but he couldn't leave the pack when his three best friends were here.

He'd always wondered what life would be like if he had the opportunity to leave the coven and find his own way, and now, he knew. He might be here because of the coven, but that didn't mean this life wasn't what he would have chosen anyway. He had Mark and a group of people who were quickly becoming close friends, and now, he had his three best friends with him.

It didn't matter what the coven was planning or what his parents thought. Lester had finally found a home and wouldn't allow anyone to take it from him.

He certainly wouldn't allow his parents or the coven elders to do so. By kicking him out of the coven and behaving the way they had, they'd given Lester more reasons to fight. He was only one mage, but he had support, and more importantly, he fought for the right reasons. He didn't want to destroy the coven to have more power or control. He didn't want to destroy the coven at all. He just wanted to be left in peace and hoped the elders would understand that.

But they'd destroyed a dragon clan, so a pack of various shifters would probably not be a problem for them.

That wasn't something Lester wanted to think about right now. The coven and the danger it represented weren't going anywhere, but Lester wasn't willing to give them more of his thoughts than he already had. It was time to truly let go, and he was ready.

"Since everyone agreed, let me call my beta and the head of pack security. You need to know them, and obviously, they need to know you're not dangerous and that you're pack members now."

Lester didn't know who Chance called, but he didn't hear any screams, so it was probably Houston. He didn't make a second call, which made Lester wonder what was happening, but he quickly found out when he heard the front door open in the distance and James bitching all the way to Chance's office.

The door swung open, and James came in, scowling. "Why do you continue welcoming people into the pack without asking me if it's a good idea?" he asked.

He stopped in front of Chance's desk and glared at him, and even though Lester was used to James's behavior by now, he still sucked in a breath and half expected Chance to tear his head off. He was pretty sure his friends felt the same way, but he told himself that they'd soon learn that Chance wasn't like other leaders and that this pack wasn't like other packs or covens.

"I'm doing what I feel is best for the pack," Chance said as if James hadn't just yelled at him.

"Who did you take in this time? You have to stop. You're not a child finding strays on the side of the road. These people are dangerous." He looked at Lester's friends. "They don't smell like shifters. Why don't they smell like shifters? And why is Lester here?"

Lester leaned back against the couch and took Mark's hand. He was going to enjoy watching the top of James's head explode.

But Chance ignored James and looked at Lester and Mark. "I already know that Lester belongs with our pack, but what about you, Mark? You didn't look convinced the last time we talked about it, so have you thought about what it might mean for you? Do you have an answer? Will you become a pack member permanently, or will we lose you?"

Mark didn't know what to do now that Chance's attention was on him. He wanted to say yes to the alpha, become a pack member, and forget he'd ever been supposed to become an alpha. All of that was behind him, and there was no going back. Even if there was, Mark wouldn't *want* to go back.

But he felt both guilty and selfish at the thought of living his life here and becoming a pack member. What about the dragons who hadn't made it? What about those who didn't have anywhere else to go and were forced to stay where the clan had lived? Mark's father had said he was planning on selling the land to a pack, but what would happen to the dragons who still lived there when he did?

Chance's expression was gentle, as if he expected Mark to break down. Mark felt like he might, but he'd been trained to hide his emotions all his life.

"You don't have to decide yet," Chance said.

"He'd better, because I don't want him around if he's not a pack member," James grumbled.

Mark sucked in a breath and waited for Chance's reaction to James's words. He knew what his father would have done if anyone had dared talk to him like that, including him. Blood would have been spilled, and his father wouldn't have regretted it.

But not Chance. He just smiled and ignored James, something that left Mark staring.

"Ignore James. He's always grumpy, even though Wade is doing his best to change that. As I said, you don't have to decide now. It would be nice to know where you stand, but I understand this kind of decision isn't easily taken, especially with the situation you left back at home."

So Chance *did* understand. He was possibly the only one who could since he was an alpha.

Mark leaned back in his chair. "I don't want to be an alpha, and I won't change my mind about that, but what about the dragons who are still out there? I haven't gone back, and my father refuses to answer my calls. I don't know what happened to most of the clan, and I don't feel right abandoning the survivors. I only know there are some, and while my father said they'd be moving away, I can't imagine all of them will."

"You feel responsible for them," Chance said.

"Wouldn't you in my place?"

"I would, so I'm not surprised." Chance glanced at James, then turned his attention back to Mark. "I want to suggest something."

"Please tell me you're not about to do what I think you're about to do," James grumbled.

Once again, Chance ignored him. "I don't like the thought of abandoning people who have no choice but to stay where they are. They don't have any protection but can't move because they have nowhere to go. I'm sure the coven will eventually reach us. If they don't already know that we welcomed you, Lester, and the others, they will soon, and when they do, we'll need all the help we can find. We have several mages now, and it would be good to have more dragons."

Mark could hardly believe what Chance was offering. "You want me to offer those dragons a place here?"

"I think it would be for the best. Your father won't stop them, since he doesn't feel responsible for them anymore, and while I understand it won't be easy for them to leave their homes, maybe a fresh start will appeal to them. We'll need to build houses, but we can do it."

That was all Mark needed. He hadn't wanted to leave those people behind, because no matter how his father had always behaved as an alpha, they had nothing to do with his decisions. They were innocent people who just wanted to live their lives.

That was what Chance was offering. Saying yes would mean that even if the dragons didn't want to move in with the pack, Mark wouldn't have to feel responsible for them. He'd give them the choice, and whatever option they chose, his involvement would be over.

"I'll find out what they want to do," he told Chance. "I can't make promises, but I'm sure some of them will want to move."

"And we'll welcome them if they do."

"Then yes, I want to be part of your pack. I want to stay with Lester and Dustin, and I want to find a place here. I don't know how much I'll be able to contribute because I've only ever been taught to be an alpha, but I'll do everything I can to show you that I can be a good pack member."

"You don't have to prove anything to me. I wouldn't be offering you this opportunity if I didn't think you could be of use to the pack and, more importantly, that you could become a productive member. Don't worry too much, Mark. I'm sure everything will be all right in the end."

Mark wanted to believe him, and it was almost easy to do so. He was a pack member now. He'd never have to worry about being an alpha and guiding people.

Chance would do it.

It was a good thing. The coven wouldn't keep their distance forever, and when they attacked, the pack would need all the support they could find. It was good that it was growing, and when the coven confronted them, Mark would be on the front line, ready to defend his alpha, his pack, and his boyfriend. He'd obey orders.

Relief over the fact that he wouldn't have to be the one giving them or making decisions made him smile.

His nightmare was over, at least in part. He would never be an alpha.

He loved that.

It was dark when he, Lester, Dustin, and Houston left Chance's house. Mark was glad Lester had convinced his friends to stay behind. They'd wanted to be with him, but there was no space in Dustin and Houston's house. Mark wanted to spend some time with Lester, and he wouldn't have been able to if his friends had come along. He wouldn't have begrudged them for it, but he had Lester all to himself tonight and couldn't wait.

"I always knew Chance would give you this opportunity," Lester said. He was rambling a bit, and it was adorable. "You shouldn't have worried so much, but I understand why you did. It's over now, though. We're both pack members."

Mark listened to every word from his boyfriend, knowing how lucky he was to have him and for both of them to be here. Mark had found a different way to keep his people safe. Maybe that was what being an alpha was about, and if it was, this was the first and only time Mark would make this kind of decision.

When the four of them had headed out, Dustin had winked at Mark before taking Houston's hand and keeping him back. They were walking behind Mark and Lester, giving them privacy. Mark had been confused, but he wasn't anymore. Dustin was trying to set him up with Lester, clearly not knowing the two of them were already together.

"I want us to spend the night together," Mark said when they reached the porch.

Lester's cheeks flushed. "We've been spending the night together a lot lately."

"That's not what I mean."

Lester bit his lower lip. "I know. I'm just not sure what to tell you." He hesitated, then looked back. Dustin and Houston weren't in sight yet, but Mark could hear them.

"I've never done *that,*" Lester said. "It doesn't mean I don't want to, but I don't know if I'm ready for it."

Mark took his hand. "We can find out together."

He pulled Lester inside the house. Lester had to know Mark would stop if he did anything that was too much for him. If he didn't, Mark would make him understand.

He didn't expect anything from Lester. He just wanted

them to be together, whatever that looked like.

He tugged Lester upstairs and headed straight for his bedroom. The two of them had been sharing since Mark had woken up. Before, Lester had been sleeping on a chair or on the edge of the bed. Since they'd kissed, they'd shared the bed, even though nothing had happened between them.

It wasn't because Mark didn't want it. It also wasn't because *Lester* didn't want it. They were taking things slow, and with so many unknowns in their lives, it felt like the right thing to do.

Mark didn't have a lot of experience with relationships. His father had forbidden him to be with anyone because he'd known that if Mark could choose, he'd choose to be with a man. He hadn't wanted the other clans to be aware of that because he'd known that if they were, they wouldn't allow Mark to marry any of their daughters.

That meant Mark's only experiences had happened in dark alleys and clubs, and he'd never had a repeat with anyone. Some nights, he'd been lucky if he even got a name.

Lester was different. He was in Mark's life to stay, and Mark wanted to take care of him. He was pretty sure Lester wanted to take care of him, too, but Mark was in control tonight.

He closed the door as soon as they were inside, then turned to Lester. He didn't know where to start, although getting both of them naked would probably be for the best.

He opened Lester's jacket, took it off, and moved to his sweater. When Mark pulled it over his head, Lester didn't try to stop him. He was wearing a t-shirt under the sweater, which was probably why.

But Mark wasn't done with him.

He didn't want to spook Lester, but he needed him more than he needed to breathe. He wanted to ask if this was how every relationship felt, but Lester had even less experience than he did, so he wouldn't know.

They didn't need experience. They just needed to be there for each other.

Mark went to his knees and got Lester to raise his feet one at a time. He took off his shoes, then his socks.

"Your turn," Lester whispered.

Mark was still wearing everything, from his boots to his jacket. He was happy to get rid of them but wasn't as careful as he'd been with Lester. He pulled off everything, abandoning them on the floor. He even took off his t-shirt, leaving only his jeans on.

Lester looked at him, then glanced away as his cheeks flushed again. Mark was pretty sure he liked what he saw, even though his skin was scarred. Mark had been through a lot, but Lester knew that. He'd been there for all of it.

"Too much?" Mark asked.

Lester shook his head. "Not enough," he whispered.

Since Mark could do something to change that, he decided to do it. He was pretty sure Lester was self-conscious, so he took off his own jeans before he finished stripping Lester. They dropped to the floor, and he didn't give them a second glance as he moved toward his boyfriend.

Lester raised his arms as Mark reached him, silently giving him what he needed. From the gesture, Mark knew that Lester wanted this, so he wouldn't have to ask.

He tugged up Lester's t-shirt, then pulled him toward the bed. Lester blinked and followed, but Mark noticed his hand skimming the top of his jeans.

"I want you naked more than I can say, but you're not entirely comfortable," Mark said.

To his surprise, Lester scowled at him. "If I was uncomfortable, I wouldn't be here. You're afraid to hurt me, but you shouldn't be. No matter how hesitant I am, I want this. I'll stop you if there's anything I don't want. I don't think I'm ready to go all the way, but I do want to get naked with you."

Mark grinned. "That's what I wanted to hear." He hooked his thumbs into his boxer briefs and pushed them down his legs.

Lester laughed, and while he was blushing, Mark could see he was already more relaxed. Maybe getting naked had been the part he'd been most afraid of. Doing so for the first time was always awkward, and while Mark didn't remember much of his first time, he knew Lester well enough to understand he wasn't entirely comfortable.

That was why he didn't touch Lester's underwear once he finally took off his jeans. He was fine with Lester still being partially dressed, even though he was already naked.

He tugged Lester onto the bed, wondering where to start. He decided that a kiss would be perfect, so as soon as Lester had settled on the mattress, that was what he did.

They'd kissed often enough that Lester didn't hesitate anymore. He moaned and pressed his almost naked body against Mark's. Mark could feel his hard cock between them. He wanted to see it but didn't want to spook Lester, so instead, he just skimmed a hand down Lester's waist. He reached around him, grabbing one of his ass cheeks, smiling when Lester sucked in a breath.

He wanted to ask if this was okay, but he already knew it was. Lester had said it—he'd stop Mark if he didn't want whatever was happening.

They kissed for what felt like forever, until Mark's cock was begging to come. He'd rather cut it off than do anything that would feel bad to Lester, so he decided to take things in hand.

He rolled Lester to his side, smacking a kiss against his shoulder when Lester squeaked. He tried to turn back, but Mark was already settling down behind him. He pressed his groin against Lester's ass, and Lester stilled, finally realizing what Mark was doing.

This was only the beginning.

Mark was pretty sure that now that they couldn't see each other anymore, Lester felt more at ease. His body relaxed, although he tensed again when Mark gently pulled down his boxer briefs. He didn't push them off, instead letting go once they were around Lester's thighs. He had what he needed.

Access to Lester's body.

Mark's cock slotted perfectly between Lester's ass cheeks. Lester sucked in a breath, but Mark wasn't done.

He'd pushed one of his arms under Lester when they'd moved, and he used his hand to skim up Lester's chest and pinch one of his nipples. Lester jerked, but Mark wasn't done.

He wrapped his fingers around Lester's cock. The moan that came from Lester told Mark he liked it. That was what Mark wanted, so he continued. His fingers never left Lester's dick, and he used his other hand to explore his boyfriend's body. He wanted to find as many sensitive spots as possible, but he could also tell it wouldn't be long before Lester came. Mark wasn't going to ask him not to. He wanted his boyfriend to feel pleasure at his hands, and the night was only just beginning.

"I don't know what to do," Lester whispered.

"You don't have to do anything. Just feel."

Lester chuckled breathlessly. "That seems too good to be true. I'm sure I should be doing something."

"Not this time. I want to do everything for you."

Not only this time, but even though Mark was pretty sure Lester was on the same page, now wasn't the right moment to ask for more.

"It feels good," Lester said with a moan.

"That's what we're aiming for," Mark said, teasing him.

He might not want to be in charge of an entire pack, but he felt more than ready to protect the one man who seemed to be perfect for him. Lester felt like he belonged in Mark's arms, and Mark hoped he felt the same. He didn't know what he'd do if that wasn't the case, but he didn't have to find out now.

Lester trembled in his arms, and Mark decided it was time to take pity on him. He squeezed Lester's cock, and at the same time, he went back up to tease his nipples. They were particularly sensitive.

Lester's groan of pleasure pushed Mark to move his hands faster. At the same time, he thrust against Lester's ass, needing the friction. Lester wouldn't be happy if he was the only one coming, and he'd insist on doing something for Mark when Mark wanted this moment to be mostly about him.

He wanted to show Lester that he was safe and that he could have whatever he wished. Whatever happened, he wanted to show him that he'd be there for him. He wanted to make him feel cherished and cared for because no one had made him feel that way.

Lester cried out and pressed his head back against Mark. Mark leaned down and kissed his neck, smiling at the way his boyfriend shuddered when he finally came.

But with Lester being Lester, he couldn't just sit back and enjoy his orgasm. As soon as he was done coming, he pressed harder against Mark, wiggling in a way that shouldn't be legal. Now that Mark didn't have to focus on Lester anymore, he could find his own pleasure, so that was what he did. Lester seemed on board with it, so Mark wouldn't feel guilty.

"This is perfect," Lester murmured.

Mark agreed, but he didn't tell him. Instead, he buried his face against Lester's neck and rutted against him until he came, spilling over Lester's ass and back.

For a moment, both of them were silent. Mark basked in the feeling of Lester pressed against him.

Until Lester said, "Are we going to end up stuck together if we stay like this for much longer? Because I have to say, it's not very comfortable. My skin is already itching."

Mark burst out laughing and buried his face against his boyfriend's hair. Life would never be boring with Lester in it, and that was exactly how Mark wanted it.

CHAPTER SEVEN

Everything was going the way it should for Lester. His three best friends had moved in with the pack, and unlike Lester, they hadn't arrived empty-handed. They'd had time to plan their escape, which meant they'd packed their things—and Lester's.

He could have cried when they handed him the first bag, and he did cry at the sight of the second. They hadn't been able to gather much because they hadn't wanted anyone to know what they were doing, but Lester now had his clothes, his phone, and some of the pictures and other mementos he'd hated losing. That was all he needed, making it much easier to settle in.

He'd never left Mark and his bedroom. Instead of moving into the bedroom that was supposed to be his in Chance and Theo's house, he was still living with Mark in Dustin's guest bedroom. They wouldn't be able to stay forever, and neither of them wanted to, but for now, this was good enough. Mark had healed, but sometimes he still got out of breath when he overworked himself, and Dustin wanted to keep an eye on him, no matter how many times Mark rolled his eyes and pointed out that he was the older brother, not Dustin.

Everything was going well, but today, something wasn't. He'd been half asleep when he'd heard Mark's phone ring, but he was fully awake now. Usually, the only people who called Mark were Dustin or other pack members. His father had never called, and Mark didn't expect him to. When Lester opened his eyes, he could see that whoever was on the phone didn't have good news.

Mark had closed his eyes, and his expression was one of sorrow. Lester wanted to reach for him, but for a moment, he didn't do anything. Sometimes, it still didn't feel real that he should be the one taking care of Mark and comforting him. He wasn't used to it but wanted to be that person, so he quickly sat up.

Mark opened his eyes. They were filling with tears, so Lester snuggled closer to him and wrapped an arm around his shoulders. Lester might be shorter, but that didn't mean Mark couldn't lean against him.

"I'm glad you managed to find me," Mark said. "I tried looking for you, but my father was less than helpful, and both yours and Rex's phones were off. I was about to come and look for you myself, but I don't know if I would have found you. You're sure you're safe?"

Lester couldn't hear the answer but felt Mark's body relax. That had to mean that whoever was on the phone was safe, but Mark still had gotten bad news.

"No, don't go to my father again. He won't be of any help. If you want, I can come pick you up."

Lester wished he could hear what was being said, but he didn't have a shifter's hearing. He could only hear Mark's answers and tried to make sense of them.

"If you're sure," Mark said. "I'll send you the address at your new number and warn the alpha that you're coming. You won't have to worry. You have a place here, just like I do."

If the situation had been different, Lester would have smiled at the thought of James having to deal with yet another new pack member. Mark seemed to care about the person on the other side of the phone, which meant they were good people, just like Mark. Chance hadn't made it a mystery that he was trying to build up pack defenses because he suspected the coven would attack eventually. They could do with more dragons. Having two was great, but having three would be even better.

Mark hung up after saying goodbye. He didn't immediately speak, and Lester gave him space. He watched as Mark opened a messaging app and quickly sent a text, but he seemed to freeze once he was done. After a moment, Lester gently took the phone out of Mark's hand, locked the screen, and put it on the bed. Then, he swung his leg over Mark's hips and settled in his lap. He put his hands on the sides of Mark's neck and rubbed his thumbs just under his jaw.

"What happened?"

Mark took a deep breath, then another. "You know I've been trying to reach my two best friends since we got here. My father couldn't tell me what happened to them, and their phones were off, probably destroyed in the fight."

Lester had noticed Mark was worried, and they'd talked about his friends. Lester had been in a similar situation when it came to his friends, so he'd understood.

But he'd gotten good news. Clearly, that wasn't the case for Mark.

"Was that one of them?" he asked.

Mark nodded. "It was Charles. He told me he'd been wounded, but he's alive. It took him some time to heal, and when he did, he tried locating both me and Rex. He couldn't find either of us, but eventually, he got my new number from my father. He also found out that Rex died."

Lester's heart hurt for his boyfriend. He didn't know Rex, but he was one of Mark's best friends, and Lester could too easily imagine the pain of losing a best friend. Even when he'd thought he'd lost all three of them, they'd still been alive.

Rex wasn't. He was gone, along with a part of Mark's heart. It would be impossible for Mark to get it back, and Lester didn't know how to help him. He couldn't tell him everything would be okay. Everything *wouldn't* be okay.

Instead, he made a soothing sound and pulled Mark closer. Mark pressed his face against Lester's neck, and when Lester felt the first tears, he held him tighter. Mark's arms came around Lester to cling to him. They had needed each other from day one, and Lester liked that it wasn't a one-way street. He needed Mark as much as Mark needed him.

But right now, he wished Mark wouldn't need him. He wished Mark's heart wasn't broken.

Eventually, Mark calmed down. Lester held him until Mark leaned away, pressing the back of his head against the headboard. Lester gave him time, but he didn't move.

"Charles is coming here," Mark said.

He opened his eyes, and at the sight of how red and puffy they were, Lester wanted to drag him back into his arms. Unfortunately, there was nothing he could do to soothe Mark's heart. Only time would do that, and even then, there would always be a wound there. Grief was complicated and personal, but Lester would do everything he could to make it easier on Mark.

"You still need to call Chance to warn him," he said gently.

Mark nodded. "I texted Charles the address, but it'll take him a few days to get here. He said he had to pack a few things and talk to people. I wouldn't be surprised if he got here with other clan members. The dragons don't know what to do. My father refuses to be the alpha he's supposed to be, and I still haven't gone back to see them. I should have."

"There's still time. You shouldn't be so hard on yourself."

Mark shook his head. "How can I not be when I lost my best friend? I wasn't there for him or the clan."

"Because my coven took you. But now that you're free, you'll be there for him. You'll be there for all of them. You might not be their alpha, but I know you. You'll make sure everyone is all right, and that makes you more responsible than your father ever was."

Mark might not believe it, but Lester would tell him as often as needed. Mark wasn't a perfect person. No one was. He didn't need to be perfect, though. He just needed to be himself and try, and Lester was sure that would be enough.

Mark wrapped his arms around Lester and held him close. "I never thought there was someone out there for me, but I'm so glad I found you," he murmured.

Lester kissed the top of his head. "There's someone for everyone. We were just lucky to find each other when we did."

About the Author

Catherine is the creator of several series, most of them paranormal, including the Whitedell Pride Series and the Gillham Pack Series. While she graduated in translation, she decided to go the writer's way because it was more fun to create her own stories and characters.

She's been living in Italy for more than twenty years, but she's a daughter of the North—Belgium to be precise—and she misses it so much that she's already planning to move back.

She loves pizza—probably too much—her son, her pets, and of course, books. She sneaks some reading time into her schedule every time she has five minutes free from writing, demands from her various pets and son, and lastly, housework.

Connect with her:

lievens.catherine@gmail.com

BookBub: https://www.bookbub.com/authors/catherine-lievens

Website: https://authorcatherinelievens.com/

Facebook: https://www.facebook.com/catherine.lievens.9

Facebook Group: https://www.facebook.com/groups/411788002341528/

Twitter: https://twitter.com/authorCLievens

Newsletter: http://eepurl.com/c-uvKn

www.ingramcontent.com/pod-product-compliance
Lightning Source LLC
LaVergne TN
LVHW012333100826
845148LV00017B/2278